"Lucas, please, I need to talk to you."

His hand tightened on the door. "We have nothing to talk about, Mia."

She glanced over her shoulder as if checking to see who might be behind her and turned back to face him. Tears stood in her eyes. "I'm in trouble, Lucas, and I have no one to turn to. Just give me five minutes of your time. That's all I'm asking."

Against his better judgment, he stepped aside and nodded. "All right. Five minutes."

He closed the door behind them and turned the thermostat up before ushering her into the living room. "Have a seat. I can see you're upset about something. So tell me about it."

Mia rubbed her hand across her eyes and sighed. "I hardly know where to start." After a moment she took a deep breath. "Did you know that Kyle was murdered?"

Lucas exhaled a deep breath. "Yes. It's been covered enough by the local media. I'm sorry, Mia. You have my condolences."

She looked up at him, and he recoiled from the anger that lined her face. "I don't need your pity, Lucas. Not now. I need help to find his killer. That's what I want you to do."

Sandra Robbins is an award-winning, multipublished author of Christian fiction who lives with her husband in Tennessee. Without the support of her wonderful husband, four children and five grandchildren, it would be impossible for her to write. It is her prayer that God will use her words to plant seeds of hope in the lives of her readers so they may come to know the peace she draws from her life.

Books by Sandra Robbins

Love Inspired Suspense

Bounty Hunters

Fugitive Trackdown
Fugitive at Large
Yuletide Fugitive Threat

The Cold Case Files

Dangerous Waters
Yuletide Jeopardy
Trail of Secrets

Final Warning
Mountain Peril
Yuletide Defender
Dangerous Reunion
Shattered Identity
Fatal Disclosure

Visit the Author Profile page at Harlequin.com.

YULETIDE
FUGITIVE
THREAT

SANDRA ROBBINS

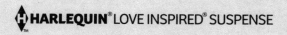

HARLEQUIN® LOVE INSPIRED® SUSPENSE

Recycling programs
for this product may
not exist in your area.

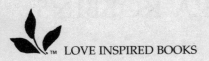

™ LOVE INSPIRED BOOKS

ISBN-13: 978-0-373-67722-1

Yuletide Fugitive Threat

Copyright © 2015 by Sandra Robbins

www.Harlequin.com

Printed in U.S.A.

Favour is deceitful, and beauty is vain: but a woman
that feareth the Lord, she shall be praised.
–Proverbs 31:30

To the memory of the 18,000 women
in the United States who have been killed by men
in domestic violence disputes since 2003.

ONE

Mia Lockhart closed her eyes as she stood on the deck of her waterfront house and listened for sounds in the dark night. The only noise that reached her ears was the soft lap of the lake as its gentle waves rippled over the rocky shoreline.

She hugged her arms around her body and shivered in the December cold. *Don't let the quiet night lull you into a false sense of security*, she said to herself. *You're not safe. Not yet.* But would she ever be? That was the question that was causing one sleepless night after another.

Try as she might, she couldn't make herself grieve over the murder of her husband a month ago. Grieving was for those with good memories of a deceased spouse, not for those who were lucky to have survived being married to a monster.

Her left hand clenched into a fist, and she flexed the arm with the broken bone that had taken so long to mend. Then she took a deep breath and exhaled. A slight smile flitted across her mouth at how much easier it was to breathe now that her ribs had healed.

No wonder she had felt no shock or sorrow when the police arrived at her door with the news of Kyle's murder. Relief, that's what had washed over her. She was finally free of the man who had controlled her life for the past seven years. Free from his possessiveness, his anger and his fists.

But she'd only been deluding herself, thinking that she'd never have to fear a man again. Freedom didn't mean she was safe, not when the accused murderer had been able to make bail and had promptly disappeared to become a fugitive from justice. Now Kyle's killer was somewhere out there, and he knew where she lived.

A gust of wind blew across the deck, and she slipped her hands into the pockets of her jacket, smiling as her fingers brushed the cell phone she'd tucked inside. Kyle had forbidden her to have a cell phone and even a landline to the house. It only made sense that her first act of freedom was to enter the digital age with a phone and a computer.

Suddenly the phone vibrated, and she tightened her grip on it. Her lips trembled as she pulled it from her pocket. An unknown number glowed on the caller ID. She knew before she answered what the voice on the line would say, but it was as if some unknown force commanded her to answer.

"H-hello," she stammered.

"Hello, Mia. It's me again."

She closed her eyes and swallowed the bile that rose in her throat. "Tony Chapman." The man who killed her husband. There was no reason to deny it. She'd known the first time he phoned right after he jumped bail.

"Why do you keep calling me? I just want to be left alone."

"I'm sure you do, and I'll be glad to do that when you give me the answers I want."

Mia's hand shook, and a tear rolled down her cheek. "I don't have any answers."

"What did you think? That you could keep it to yourself for a Christmas present from your dearly departed husband?" he growled. "If that's what you thought, then you're wrong. Dead or alive, he still owes me, and I intend to collect. So if you think you're going to keep it to yourself, you have another think coming."

"Keep what for myself?" she screamed into the phone.

"Calm down, Mia. All you have to do is tell me where it is, and you'll never hear from me again."

Her body was shaking with sobs by this time. "I don't know what *it* is. And even if I did, Kyle would never have told me anything about his business. Now, please, leave me alone."

"Dream on!" he shouted. "I'm through being nice. Tell me what I want to know, or you're going to be sorry."

"I'm sorry already! Sorry I ever met Kyle Lockhart and sorry I have no idea what you're talking about. If I did, I'd give it to you."

Tony was quiet for a moment. "Maybe you don't know what he did with it. But if you think very carefully, you might be able to remember something he said or did. Maybe he had a place where he kept his secrets."

"Kyle had lots of secrets, but he never shared them with me. Now I'm warning you. I've had all of these phone calls I can stand. I'm going to the police to turn this matter over to them. Maybe they know where Kyle hid whatever it is you're looking for."

"If you know what's good for you, you'll stay away from the police, or you'll end up like Kyle, with three bullet holes in your head."

Mia shook so badly she could hardly hold the phone to her ear. "Leave me alone!" she screamed.

"Not until I get what's mine. So you'd better watch out, lady. I'm coming after you."

The call ended, and she pulled the phone away from her ear. What was this all about? It wouldn't surprise her if Kyle had been involved in something illegal that had gotten him killed, but she knew nothing about it. In fact, she knew next to nothing about his life outside of this house that he'd made her prison.

Sliding the phone back into her pocket, she turned to go back inside but stopped, her eyes growing wide. A light like a tiny flame flared at the edge of the tree line near the lake and then disappeared, to be replaced by a small red glow. She squinted into the darkness and then backed away, shaking her head in denial.

She'd seen a flicker of fire that had lit a cigarette, and now whoever was smoking it stood just a few feet away as he watched her on the deck. A mewling sound of distress erupted from her mouth, and she dashed back into the house, locking the door behind her.

As she ran into the bedroom, she glanced at the clock on the bedside table: 2:30 a.m. It would be hours before the sun was up, and she couldn't stay here until then. She didn't know where she could go, but she had to get out of this house. Get away from the nightmare that had taken over her life.

She jerked a pair of jeans and a sweater from the closet and dressed as quickly as she could. Then, pulling on her coat and grabbing her purse and cell phone, she headed to the kitchen where she always hung the car keys on the hook by the door.

As she stepped into the kitchen, her gaze lit on the rack, and her stomach did a somersault. No key ring. She came to an abrupt halt and frowned. Where was it?

A sickening feeling washed over her as the answer came to her. The keys weren't on the hook because they were in her purse, where she'd placed them after a trip to the grocery store. She hadn't hung the key ring back in place because she hadn't come in through the garage. The automatic garage door opener wasn't working, so she'd left the car in the driveway.

And that's where it was now. Sitting in the driveway. In the dark. Where someone was watching from the shadows of the woods. Did she dare go outside and face being attacked? Or did she stay inside and hope he didn't decide to break in? Either choice left a lot to be desired.

Every nerve ending in her body screamed that she had to do something, and before she even realized it, the decision had been made. She jerked the key ring from her purse, opened the front door and ran for the car.

She'd just grabbed the door handle when an arm circled her neck, and the tip of the knife in her attacker's other hand pressed against her carotid artery. The smell of cigarette smoke filled her nostrils. She held her breath and tried to pull free, but the arm tightened.

A soft chuckle drifted to her ear as a warm breath fanned the side of her face. "Don't waste your energy, sweetheart. You're not getting away from me."

His voice sounded deeper than it had on the phone, more sinister and full of evil. She tried to suppress the whimper rising in her throat, but it was no use. He knew how scared she was, and that was his advantage over her.

"Let me go!" she begged. "I can't give you what you want because I don't know what you're talking about."

"We'll see about that. I think by the time I

get through with you, you'll be begging to tell me all of your secrets."

The tone of his voice had grown harder, just like Kyle's used to when he told her he would never have hurt her if she hadn't provoked him into doing it. After a while she had come to believe him. She'd given in, gone along with whatever he wanted—even when all he seemed to want was a punching bag. But she would not give in to this man, nor would she let him take her anywhere. If she did, she had no doubt she would end up dead just like Kyle.

If she had never been strong in her life, she had to be now. Only a desperate move could get her out of this killer's clutches. Thankfully she hadn't dropped her car keys when she'd been attacked, and she tightened her grip on them. If she could free herself of Tony's arm around her throat, she might be able to jump in the car and drive away.

Taking a deep breath to calm her racing heart, she closed her fingers around the small canister of pepper spray dangling from the key ring she'd bought after he'd called her the first time. In a few moments she would either be free or stabbed to death in her driveway.

In one quick motion she raised the canister and sprayed the contents over her shoulder into

Tony Chapman's face. His agonized cry split the night air, and his grip on her loosened as he stumbled backward.

Those few seconds were enough time for her to pull the car door open, jump inside and roar down the driveway. As she raced down the road leading to the main highway, she kept a watch in the rearview mirror, but no one followed her.

She didn't slow down until she turned onto I-240 for the short drive into Memphis. Her mind whirled with questions about what she was going to do. She had no friends. Nowhere to turn. Where could she go?

And then she straightened in her seat as the answer popped into her head. A bounty hunter, that's what she needed. Someone who could track Tony Chapman down and return him to custody. And it so happened she had once known someone who now did that for a living. Lucas Knight. But she hadn't seen Lucas in seven years. And the last time she'd seen him, he'd said he never wanted to lay eyes on her again.

A lot of time had passed, she reasoned with herself. He'd moved on. She'd seen him on TV just a few weeks ago, giving an interview with his brother and sister about the Knight Fugitive Recovery Agency, the family's bounty hunter business. He'd looked good—great, actually. The interviewer had said their agency had the best reputation for bringing in bail jumpers of any group in the city. But would Lucas help her?

The lights of an all-night diner off the highway caught her attention, and she exited and pulled to a stop near the front entrance. Only three other cars sat in the parking lot at 3:00 a.m. Evidently someone else had trouble sleeping at night.

She had a few hours before she could go see Lucas, and she needed to use that time to decide how she was going to persuade him to help a woman whom he had once said he would hate until the day he died. This diner offered the perfect place for her to sit and ponder how in the world she was ever going to convince Lucas to track down Tony Chapman and return him to custody.

She took a deep breath, stepped from the car and walked toward the diner's entrance.

Lucas Knight woke to a pounding at his front door. He sat up in bed, glanced at the bedside clock and groaned: 6:00 a.m. His brother, Adam, had said he'd be by early to pick him up for the trip they were taking to Nashville, but he hadn't thought he meant *this* early.

Muttering to himself, Lucas climbed out of bed and jerked on his jeans and the sweatshirt he'd draped across the bedroom chair before going to bed last night. If Adam thought he was going to hurry him into going before he'd had his coffee and showered, he wasn't as smart as he thought he was.

The pounding increased, and he stormed across the living room floor and jerked the front door open. "Adam, what do you mean…"

His words died in his throat, and all he could do was stare in surprise at Mia Fletcher standing in front of him. He shook his head. No, Mia Lockhart. That had become her name after she'd walked out on him for the man her daddy had picked for her.

He grabbed the side of the door and hung on so that he didn't collapse right in front of her. What was she doing standing on his porch at six o'clock in the morning?

His gaze swept her, and he swallowed the tiny glimmer of pleasure at seeing her. She was just as beautiful as ever. Even though she wore no makeup and her long blond hair was pulled up in a practical ponytail, she had that fresh-scrubbed look he'd always liked. What he didn't like was the hint of fear in her blue eyes. She stared at him apprehensively, as if to say she had no idea how he would react at her sudden appearance.

He wouldn't allow himself to be glad to see her. Couldn't allow it. It had taken too long to get over her, and he wasn't about to revisit those old memories and the scars they had left deep inside of him. He should slam the door in her face and forget she'd ever come here. He started to do that, but she spoke before he could.

"Lucas, please, I need to talk to you."

His hand tightened on the door. "We have nothing to talk about, Mia."

She glanced over her shoulder, as if checking to see who might be behind her, and turned back to face him. Tears stood in her eyes. "I'm in trouble, Lucas, and I have no one to turn to. Just give me five minutes of your time. After that, if you won't help me, I'll go away and never bother you again. Five minutes. That's all I'm asking."

She shivered and clutched her jacket tighter around her. For the first time he noticed the chill in the air. The temperature had to be in the thirties, and she looked as if she was chilled to the bone. Against his better judgment, he stepped aside and nodded.

"All right. Five minutes. I'll give you that."

She brushed past him, and the scent of the fruity shampoo she'd always used filled his nostrils. The memory of that smell had kept him awake many nights when he was still a navy SEAL, but he'd never thought he'd experience it firsthand again.

He closed the door behind them and turned the thermostat up before ushering her into the living room. "Have a seat."

She sank down on the sofa and rubbed her hands together before she offered him a weak smile. "It feels good in here. I must have stood on your porch for fifteen minutes trying to get up my nerve to knock. It was colder than I thought."

He pressed his lips together and didn't say anything, but his gaze drifted down to her hands, which she was still rubbing together. No sign of a wedding ring.

She shivered again, and he refocused his thoughts. A good host would offer her a cup of coffee, but he was in no mood to make this any easier. The quicker he could get Mia out of here, the better off he'd be.

He took a deep breath. "Five minutes, you said. So, what has brought you to my door so early in the morning?" He paused for a moment and frowned. "Wait a minute. I haven't seen or heard from you in seven years. How did you know where I live? I bought this house after I got out of the navy. You've never been here before."

Her cheeks flushed even more. "I was going to come to your office, but I decided I couldn't wait that long to see you. I had to leave home quickly in the middle of the night, and I've spent the last three hours in an all-night diner. I used my phone to look up your address online."

For the first time he noticed her red-streaked eyes and the dark circles underneath on her skin. "Have you been up all night?"

She nodded.

Lucas sat down in a chair facing the sofa and placed his hands on his knees. "Okay. I can see you're upset about something. So tell me about it."

Mia rubbed her hand across her eyes and sighed. "I hardly know where to start." After a moment she took a deep breath. "Did you know that Kyle was murdered?"

Lucas exhaled a deep breath. "Yes. It's been covered enough by the local media. 'Kyle Lockhart, respected antiques authority and honored young leader in the local arts community, found brutally murdered in an apparent burglary of his office at Shackleford's Imports,' I believe is how the newscasters on TV stated it." He regretted his mocking words when he saw her eyes fill again. He swallowed and spoke in a gentler tone. "I'm sorry, Mia. You have my condolences."

She looked up at him, and he recoiled from the anger that lined her face. "I don't need your pity, Lucas. Not now. I need help to find his killer. That's what I want you to do."

He shook his head and stood up. "The paper said the police had arrested somebody. If it's true that they have enough evidence for a conviction, then the case is closed. The killer will be found guilty, and you can move on, living the life of a rich widow."

"Rich widow? Is that what you think of me?" she screamed as she jumped to her feet. "I would love to get on with my life, but, unfortunately, I can't. Tony Chapman, who was arrested for killing Kyle, was able to make bail, after which he ran. As far as the authorities are concerned, he's disappeared. But he hasn't. He's terrorizing me and making my life miserable."

Her outburst stunned Lucas, and he frowned. "What do you mean he's terrorizing you?"

She sank back to the couch and closed her

eyes for a moment. "A few days after Tony jumped bail, I began getting phone calls from him demanding to know where Kyle had hidden *it*. I told him I had no idea what he was talking about, but he didn't believe me. The phone calls have gotten worse, and tonight he came to my house and attacked me. I only got away because I had a canister of pepper spray on my key ring."

Lucas stared at Mia and tried to process what she'd just told him. "Mia, I don't know what to say."

She scooted to the edge of the sofa and stared at him, her eyes pleading with him for help. "I need help, Lucas. I want to hire you to find him. He's a fugitive, and you're a bounty hunter. If you can bring him in, then maybe I can put this whole crazy ordeal behind me."

Work for her? She wanted that after everything that had happened between them? He pushed to his feet, walked over to the window and stared outside. He couldn't help her. It would stir up too many memories that he had safely stored away, and he didn't need to be reminded. But he had to admit, she needed help.

Finally he turned back to her and shook his head. "I'm sorry, Mia. I don't think it would be a good idea for me to work for you. But I'm sure Adam would be glad to do it."

Her eyebrows arched. "Adam?"

"Yes. You remember my older brother. He takes cases like this all the time. Why don't you come by our office later today…?" A sudden thought hit him, and he shook his head. "No, he won't be in today. We're going to Nashville. Maybe you could come tomorrow."

She stared at him for a moment before she slowly rose to her feet. "No. I can't wait that long."

"Then what about Jessica? She's going to be in the office today. I'm sure she would be glad to help you."

She shook her head. "That's all right, Lucas. If you won't help me, I'll have to figure out another way to get through this."

The words, spoken without any emotion, hit Lucas as if his heart was being ripped from his body. He watched as she took a step to leave, but he felt powerless to stop her. She had almost reached the front door into the entryway when her cell phone rang. She stopped and pulled it from her pocket. Her eyes grew wide, and she began to shake.

"He's calling again!" she moaned. "Why won't he leave me alone?"

Lucas was at her side in two strides and jerked the phone from her hand. "Hello! Who is this?" he yelled into the phone.

There was a short pause before a soft chuckle sounded. "Hello. Mr. Knight, I assume. Tell Mia that running to you isn't going to help her any. You can't be with her every minute, and the next time I get my hands on her, I'll gladly cut her throat without hesitation."

"You'll what?" But there was no answer. The man had already disconnected the call. Lucas handed the phone back to Mia. "He'll cut your throat? What's that about? You didn't say anything about a knife."

Her forehead wrinkled. "I didn't? That was when he caught me trying to get in my car. He was holding a knife to my throat when I sprayed him with the pepper spray."

Lucas's mouth dropped open. "Do you realize that his reflex action could have left you stabbed and bleeding to death?"

She nodded. "I did. But doing nothing would have been worse. I knew I couldn't be his victim." She clenched her fists and pounded them against the sides of her legs. "I don't want to be anybody's victim anymore."

Something in the way she said it sent warning signals flashing in his mind. Maybe there was more to Mia's situation than she was telling. If so, he wanted to find out what it was. He stuck his hands in his jeans pockets and rocked back on his heels.

"Are you hungry, Mia?"

"Yeah, a little. I think I drank about five cups of coffee while I was in that diner, but I couldn't eat anything."

He smiled. "Would you like some breakfast? I still know my way around the kitchen."

Her body relaxed, and she smiled the first real smile he'd seen since she arrived. "You always were the best cook I'd ever known."

His skin warmed, and he couldn't help but grin at the compliment. "It was one of my many talents," he joked. "If I'm going to take your case, I need to find out all the details, and I always work better on a full stomach. Go on in the kitchen. I need to call Adam and leave a message for him. Then I'll see what I can rustle up for us to eat."

He swept his arm in the direction of the kitchen, and she smiled before she headed there. He closed his eyes for a moment and bit down on his lip. What would Adam say when he told him why he was canceling on their trip to Nashville? Especially when his brother found out that Lucas had just accepted Mia Lockhart as a new client at the Knight Agency. After a moment he shrugged. It didn't matter.

Mia had shown up on his doorstep looking like a lost waif. It didn't take a rocket scientist to figure out that she was in a lot of trouble and needed help. If he could help her, that's what he needed to do. He'd never forgive himself if he sent her away and then learned from the news that she'd been hurt, or killed.

But finding the bail jumper was all this was going to be. She was hiring him for a job. After it was over, she would pay him, and he'd never have to see her again. That's the way he wanted it, and that's the way it was going to be.

TWO

Thirty minutes later Mia sat across the kitchen table from Lucas and stared down at the plate in front of her. "This is delicious. I haven't had an omelet in a long time, and you always made the best," she said.

He nodded and finished chewing his last bite before he spoke. "I still like to cook, but I don't advertise it to any of the guys in my biker club. I don't think I could take the jokes they'd make about me in the kitchen."

She laughed and arched an eyebrow. "So you're still riding a motorcycle?"

He shrugged. "Yeah. It gives me something to do when I'm off work, which isn't very often."

"I suppose your mother is still as concerned about your dangerous hobby as ever," she said as she scooped another bite onto her fork. "By the way, how are your parents? I always liked them."

She sensed a sudden chill in the friendly atmosphere and sat back in her chair. "Is something wrong, Lucas?"

He raised his head and stared at her, his eyes dark and foreboding. "If I'm going to take your case, I think we need to get something straight right off."

She laced her fingers together in her lap and gripped them tightly. "A-all r-right. What is it?"

He leaned forward, a frown creasing his forehead. "I think it would be better if we don't mention our past relationship. There's no need to revisit ancient history, whether it's talking about what I used to cook, my parents or whatever. This is strictly business. You're hiring me to do a job for you. I'll do it, and you'll pay me when it's over. Can you agree to that?"

She struggled to keep her voice steady as she answered him. "I can, but if you're going to take my case, then there's something I need to tell you."

He tilted his head to one side and eyed her suspiciously. "What is it?"

"I know your services don't come cheap, and I will pay you. It just may take some time. Kyle's lawyer is in the process of untangling all his business dealings. I've been allowed to stay in the house for a while. Although it's the last place I want to be, I don't have anywhere else to go until the estate is settled. I have very little money. I thought you should know."

Lucas stared at her for a moment before he set his coffee cup down and leaned toward her. "I can understand about the will not being settled. But what about your money?"

Her eyes grew wide. "What money?"

"That you make from your job."

"I don't have a job. I've never had one."

His mouth gaped open, and he blinked his eyes. "All you ever wanted to do was to own a dance studio and teach children ballet. You studied for years. What happened?"

Her stomach was beginning to roil at all his questions, and she jumped to her feet and grabbed her plate. She walked to the garbage disposal and shoveled her leftover food into the sink before she turned back around. "I thought this was going to be strictly business," she retorted. "Do you need to know to solve the case? The studio never happened—end of story."

He stepped closer to her. "Fine, then. What about your father? If you don't have enough money to live on until the estate is settled, couldn't he help you?"

She shook her head but didn't turn around to face him. "My father died three years ago. He and Kyle got along great." Much better than *she* had ever gotten along with her distant, disapproving father. "So much so that he made Kyle the executor of his estate. My lawyer told me I'll be able to get that inheritance back, but it's going to take a while."

"I'm sorry. I didn't know about your father. But what about friends? Could they help you?"

Mia clenched her fists and gritted her teeth before she whirled and faced Lucas. "No! Don't you understand? I'm not like you, Lucas. I don't have a family that cares what happens to me, and I don't have friends who want to help me." Tears welled in her eyes. "When I was racking my brain trying to think who I could go to for help, you were the only one who came to mind. A college boyfriend that I hadn't seen in seven years. You probably haven't given me a thought in years, and yet you were the only one I felt like I could turn to for help."

She covered her face with her hands and began to sob. After a few moments, Lucas reached out and patted her arm. "I'm sorry," he said. "I didn't mean to make you cry."

He reached for her napkin and stuck it in her hand. She began to wipe the tears from her face and shake her head. "No, I'm the one who's sorry. I shouldn't have gone to pieces like that, but I've been so scared ever since those phone calls started. I knew you were my only hope of getting anything done. Will you please help me, Lucas?"

The look on his face told her he still wasn't pleased about the prospect. "I'll take the job of tracking Tony Chapman. After all, that's what we're in business for, bringing in fugitives from justice. But I can't guarantee how long it will take me."

Mia wiped her eyes again. "It can't be soon enough for me. I want to try and get on with my life."

"I hope it won't take long either. But for now, I need some information from you. Why don't we take our coffee in the living room, and you can fill me in on all the details about Kyle?"

She blew her nose and smiled through her tears. "Okay."

They walked back to the living room and settled on the sofa, their cups in their hands. Mia pulled her knees up and curled into the corner of the sofa, so she could sit facing him. He reached for a notebook that was lying on the coffee table, flipped it open and pulled a pen out. "Now, tell me about Kyle's job."

She wrapped her hand around the mug and thought for a moment before she answered.

"Kyle went to work at Shackleford Imports right after we were married. They sell antiques and antiquities in their showroom, as well as working with clients on arranging special purchases. Kyle was the import/export manager. It was his job to oversee the paperwork and the monetary transactions on all the international acquisitions, as well as working with customs agents on all items coming into or leaving the country. He also handled special clients for the company."

Lucas wrote as she talked and didn't look up as he asked his next question. "It sounds like an important job. I assume he was paid well."

"He was. I don't really know how much—he handled all our finances—but he told me once it was in the six figures."

Lucas gave a low whistle. "The owner must have thought he did a good job to pay that well."

Mia shrugged. "I suppose so. Mr. Shackleford has been ill for the past year and a half, and Kyle was basically running the business."

"Did the other employees like him?"

"I don't know."

He glanced up at her answer and then directed his gaze back to his note-taking. "And why is that?"

"Because I never got to know any of them very well."

Lucas slowly raised his head to stare at her, a frown wrinkling his forehead. "Shackleford's is well-known in the city. There are stories in the paper all the time about events they're having to show a new acquisition or the opening of some exhibit they've come up with. He worked there for seven years, Mia. Didn't you go with him to any of the events?"

She shook her head. "A few times when we first married, but that soon ended. He thought I couldn't hold my own in conversation with the intellectual people who frequented the events. So he quit taking me."

He opened his mouth to speak but then seemed to think better of it. He cleared his throat and looked back down at the notebook. "The police arrested Tony Chapman for Kyle's murder. Did you know him?"

"No, I'd never heard of him, until he was arrested. Then a few days later I was notified he had made bail. And soon after that, he disappeared. Except he started calling me all the time."

"And you have no idea what it is he thinks Kyle has hidden from him?"

She shook her head and frowned. "I can't

imagine what it is. Kyle never talked to me about his business dealings in any kind of detail. Everything he told me was very general. I don't even know if he and Tony had business dealings. I'm beginning to wonder if it wasn't something illegal. And if there was a falling-out with them, and that's why Tony killed him."

Lucas nodded. "That's a logical explanation, but I don't guess we'll know for sure until I can find Tony." He paused a moment and then looked at her again. "There are lots of unanswered questions about this whole case."

"I know."

"One of them is, how did Tony know you had come to see me today? When I answered the phone, he called me by name—he knew you were with me. Did you see a car following you when you drove here? Or did one drive by after you parked in front of my house?"

She shook her head and yawned. "No. I checked all the way. And when I left the diner, I took a lot of back streets to get here. It was so late, the streets were empty—I'd have noticed if someone was following me. There was no one behind me, and no one drove by after I arrived here."

Lucas closed the notebook and reached for her coffee cup. "Would you like a refill?"

"That would be nice."

He laid the notebook on the coffee table and walked from the room. Mia scooted down on the couch, stretched her legs out and snuggled into the soft cushions. The stress of the past few weeks had left her tense and wary, but for some reason she felt safer now than she had in years.

She'd made the right decision. If anyone could help her, Lucas could, and he'd seemed understanding about her lack of funds at the present time. She had no illusions about how he felt about her. He still hated her. She could see it in his eyes. But he was willing to help her, and that was all she needed. Someone she trusted who could put a stop to the terror in her life.

With a sigh she closed her eyes and drifted into a deep sleep.

Lucas walked back into the living room and stopped at the door. A soft snore came from Mia's prone figure sprawled on the couch. She had to be dead on her feet after the night she'd had. He set the cup of coffee down and reached for an afghan draped across a chair next to the sofa.

As he covered her with the colorful blanket, he thought of his mother and the hours she'd spent crocheting this beautiful afghan and how thrilled she'd been when she saw how he liked it. He spread it over Mia's body and pulled it up around her shoulders.

Then he stepped back and stared down at her. He still couldn't believe she was here. Asleep on his sofa. And just as attractive as she'd been when they were in college.

He shook his head and took a step back. No use thinking that way. What was between them had died seven years ago when she chose Kyle instead of him. And nothing was going to change that.

He turned around and strode again to the kitchen, where he began to put the breakfast dishes in the dishwasher. As he worked, he recalled all the things Mia had said while they were eating. Some things didn't make sense.

Mia had always been vivacious and energetic and enjoyed being with people. How had she ended up with no friends? Less surprising was that she had no family. When they'd been dating, her father was all the family she had, and their relationship had always been tense.

It hadn't taken him long when they were in college to find out how her father controlled her life, from what she wore to the friends she had. Her one attempt at rebelling against her father's authority had been when she'd told him she was going to marry Lucas. But that resolve hadn't lasted very long. She and Lucas had had a fight over the fact that he wanted to wait until he'd finished his SEAL training before marrying her. Lucas had thought that they'd be able to work things out once he got back from basic training...but by then, she'd already married another man—one who had her father's stamp of approval.

Lucas closed the dishwasher, sat down at the kitchen table and pulled out his cell phone. He punched in the number for Scottie Murray, the computer whiz they used at the agency, and waited for him to answer. Lucas had no idea how Scottie could find even the deepest buried items on the internet with little effort. But then again, he didn't ask. It was better if he didn't know some of Scottie's secrets.

Scottie connected on the third ring. "Hello."

"Scottie, Lucas Knight here."

"Hey, man. What's up?"

"I have a new client. I need you to do some digging for me."

"Sure. What do you want?"

"I want you to find me everything you can on a man named Kyle Lockhart and his wife, Mia. Lockhart was murdered about a month ago, and

I need a full background search on him. Let me know the minute you find out anything."

"Okay, dude. You got it. I'll get to work right away."

Lucas disconnected the call and sat at the table, thinking for a few minutes. If there was more to Mia's story than what she was telling him, Scottie would find it. He glanced at the clock on the wall: 8:00 a.m. Scottie might not call back for several hours. That gave him time to take care of other things.

He pulled out his cell phone and dialed Adam's number. It went to voice mail right away. Without giving details, he left a short message that he wouldn't be able to go to Nashville and would explain later. Then he headed to the shower.

An hour later he walked back into the living room to check on Mia. She still lay there sound asleep but had pulled the cover up around her neck more. He watched her even breathing for a moment, before he turned and walked back to the kitchen.

He'd just entered the room when his phone rang. He pulled the phone from his pocket and smiled at Scottie's name on the screen.

"Hey, Scottie. Did you find something for me?"

"Yeah, I did. And some of it's very interesting. This Lockhart guy was quite a character. I have everything in a file that I just emailed to you. There's probably more, but I thought this would give you something to study while I keep digging into his life."

"Thanks, Scottie. Let me know when you have more."

As he disconnected the call, Lucas strode toward his office to turn on his computer. Within seconds he had opened his email and found the file Scottie had sent.

Carefully, he began to read through the pages contained in the report. The first ones dealt with Kyle's job at the import business. There was a job description, some evaluations filled out by the owner and some letters of commendation from community leaders.

Those were followed by newspaper articles reporting Kyle's important acquisitions and pictures of him at events, a wineglass in his hand, and surrounded by beautiful women, smiling for the cameras. As Lucas studied picture after picture, he discovered the same woman was in each one. The captions underneath identified her as Christine Abbott, heiress to her family's hotel chain.

Was it coincidence that Christine was in all

the photos? He doubted it, but that was something Lucas could pursue later.

He scrolled to the next page of the file. His eyes grew wide as a police report came into view. Lucas leaned closer to the computer screen and read, his stomach churning as he realized what he was looking at. A report of Kyle Lockhart's arrest, six months before his death, for domestic abuse.

Lucas's fingers shook as he read the account. Teenagers having a party on the shore of the lake near Mia's house had called the police to report hearing screams. The police had arrived to find Mia Lockhart severely injured. She had been transported to a hospital where it was determined she had a broken arm and several broken ribs, along with cuts and bruises over most of her face.

Lucas scrolled down further and gasped aloud when a picture of a bruised and battered Mia appeared on the screen. He clamped his hand over his mouth to keep from crying out as he read that Mia had refused to press charges.

Before he knew what he was doing, he had dialed Scottie's number. He answered on the first ring.

"Scottie, did you see the picture of Lockhart's wife?"

"Yeah, man. I saw it. But that's just one of many."

"What do you mean by that?"

"The investigating cop is a guy I know, so I called him and asked him about Lockhart. He said that everybody at the precinct knew Mia Lockhart was a victim of repeated domestic abuse. They tried to get her to press charges every time he put her in the hospital, but she never would. My friend said that's the way victims are. Their abuser convinces them that they deserve what they're getting. Most of them have nowhere else to go, so they stay. It's sad, isn't it?"

Lucas's breath hitched in his throat. "Yeah. Real sad. Thanks, Scottie."

For a few minutes after disconnecting the call Lucas sat still and thought about what he'd discovered. No wonder Mia had no one to turn to. She'd been the victim of the one person who was supposed to take care of her.

He stood and walked back into the living room where she still lay sleeping. She moaned and clenched her fingers around the top of the afghan as she pulled it tighter around her neck.

"No," she murmured as her body twitched. "I'm sorry."

He had no idea what she was dreaming, but he knew for a certainty now that her life had been a nightmare. And when her husband was killed, she'd ended up in a new nightmare, threatened and eventually assaulted by the man who'd murdered Kyle. She had come to him for help, and he would do everything he could to find the man who'd terrorized her for the past few weeks.

As for Kyle Lockhart, there was nothing Lucas could do about him now. But just maybe he could bring some closure to Mia for what she had experienced at her husband's hands. If he could do that, maybe he, too, could at last put some closure to the most painful period of his life.

Mia slowly opened her eyes and stretched her arms over her head. She didn't know when she'd slept so soundly. Her fingers brushed against the soft yarn at her neck, and she looked down at the afghan covering her from her shoulders to her toes. She trailed her fingers down the crocheted diagonal lines of muted shades of green, brown and gray that blended in with the earthy tones of Lucas's house. Her eyes flew open wide at the thought of his name.

Lucas! She was in his house. Asleep on his sofa.

"Are you finally awake?"

His voice came from the direction to her left. She bolted upright on the sofa and jerked her head around to stare at him. The sun shone through the window behind him and cast shadows across the chair where he sat. He had his ankle propped on the opposite leg and sat there staring at her, the expression on his face unreadable.

She clutched the afghan tighter around her neck and swallowed. "Lucas. You scared me."

His hands clenched around the arms of the chair, but he didn't rise. "Did I? I'm sorry. I was beginning to wonder if you were ever going to wake up."

She swiveled her body around until her feet were on the floor, and she sat facing him. "I guess I was more tired than I thought. I'm sorry if I inconvenienced you by sleeping here. What time is it?"

"It's close to three o'clock. You must have been really tired."

She shook her head in disbelief. "I'm so

sorry, Lucas. I hope I didn't keep you from going to work."

"I have an office here. I had some paperwork I took care of, so it was no problem."

She pushed to her feet and busied herself folding the afghan. "I'll get out of here. Thank you for everything today. I'll give you my cell phone number so you can contact me when you have any news about Tony Chapman."

She reached to put the afghan on the back of the sofa, but she froze at the sharp words he uttered. "And where are you going?"

His voice had a hoarse rasp to it. Was that anger she heard? Or was she so used to hearing Kyle's harsh tone that she looked for it in everyone she encountered? She bit her lip and laid the afghan down before she turned to face him. "I don't know yet, but I'll let you know when I get settled, maybe in a hotel."

"I thought you didn't have any money."

She frowned. What was with the interrogation? She swallowed hard and tried to remain calm. "I have a little. I think I can afford a cheap motel."

He pushed to his feet and took a step toward her. He stuck his hands in his pockets and stared at her without blinking. "I have a few questions before you leave."

"Okay."

He advanced, and she inched backward until her legs bumped the sofa, and she sank onto it. Lucas took a deep breath as he towered over her. "I need to know more about Kyle, so I can figure out what might have made someone want to kill him. You said he isolated you from friends, he wouldn't let you work, and in the past few years, he never took you with him to business events. Other than that, how did he treat you?"

Her fingers shook, and she laced them together to hold them still. "H-he was my husband. H-he treated me like I was his wife."

Lucas's steel blue eyes bored into hers, and she dropped her gaze. "And what does that mean? Was he kind? Did he make you happy? Did he love you?"

Her face burned from his intense gaze, and she cast a furtive glance down at her hands. "Lucas, I don't see what this has to do with finding the man who killed him."

With a sigh, he sat on the sofa next to her. When she peeked over at him, she saw him staring down at his feet for a moment before he reached over, pulled one of her hands loose from the other and wrapped his fingers around hers. She started to draw away from him, but he tightened his grip. She opened her mouth to protest, but the sad look in his eyes stopped her. "It's all right, Mia," he said, his gentle tone piercing the barricades around her heart. "I know what kind of love he gave you. So tell me the truth."

For a moment she couldn't respond. Her mouth trembled as she realized that for years, there'd been nobody she could tell. Now a man who had been kinder to her than any other in her entire life was asking for the truth. She couldn't refuse, but when she opened her mouth to speak, the words wouldn't come. A keening wail drifted from her throat, and she closed her eyes as the tears began to stream down her face. She took a deep breath.

"All right!" she sobbed. "My marriage was a nightmare. Kyle was a monster, and I lived in fear that every day would be the one when he would finally go too far and kill me."

She felt him move closer, and she glanced up just as he reached out and patted her shoulder. That only produced more tears. "Why didn't you come to me?" he whispered. "I would have helped you."

The sorrow in his eyes pierced her heart, and she pulled free of him and turned her face into the soft afghan she'd just folded minutes before.

He didn't say anything as she sobbed but patted her shoulder from time to time and uttered some soothing words.

After several minutes she sat up and wiped at her eyes. Her pulse was still racing, but it was freeing to finally admit to someone what her life had been like. And she was glad Lucas was the one she could tell.

"After Kyle and I were married, I discovered very quickly why my father had wanted me to marry him. He was like my father, but worse. He didn't allow me to make any decisions, not even about the clothes I wore. He picked out everything, provided everything and wanted me at home when he got there. The abuse wasn't too bad at first. If I displeased him, didn't cook a meal the way he liked it, he would slap me. Then one night things escalated."

"What happened?"

"He was watching the news, and the reporter did a story about your brother, Adam, bringing in a fugitive wanted in a high-profile case. Adam told about the Knight Agency, and he mentioned that his younger brother was serving in the navy SEALs but was arriving home on leave soon. I made the mistake of saying that I was glad you had pursued your goal, and Kyle went wild. He accused me of still being in love with you and of plotting to meet you when you came home on leave. That's the first night I had to go to the hospital."

Lucas's Adam's apple bobbed, and he swallowed hard. "I'm sorry," he whispered.

She waved her hand in dismissal. "It wasn't your fault. I'd made the mistake of marrying him. After that, though, things got worse."

"Why didn't you leave?"

She shrugged. "I tried to once, but he found me and brought me back. That was one of the worst beatings. He told me if I ever left again, he'd kill me. He hired a maid after that to keep tabs on me. She reported every little thing I did to Kyle."

Lucas squeezed her hand tighter and then released it. "I'm so sorry you had to endure this. I wish I could have helped you."

"It's okay, Lucas. I've been alone for so long that I don't expect much from anybody anymore." Her eyes filled with tears, and she could barely make out his image even though he sat next to her. "But, please, help me now. I'm never going to be free of Kyle and the life he made me live until his killer is caught."

He smiled at her, and for the first time in years she felt some hope. Maybe she could overcome the fear she'd lived in for so long.

"Don't worry, Mia. I'll help you, and I promise I'll do everything in my power to find this guy and keep you safe from him."

Her eyes filled with tears again. "I was so afraid to come here. I didn't know if you'd even listen to me. I can never tell you how much I appreciate your help."

Telling Lucas about her life hadn't been easy, but she felt better, almost as if a dam had burst and all the memories that threatened her sanity had poured out. Maybe this was the beginning of a new life for her. She hoped so.

She had no idea what she'd do once Tony Chapman was back in jail where he belonged, but at least she'd be free. Free to go and do as she pleased. And free of everything that tied her to the past. And Lucas was going to make that happen.

THREE

Lucas walked to the window in the living room and stared outside. The discovery of what Mia's marriage had been like had almost sucked the breath out of him. He raked his hand through his hair and groaned. Even if he had spent the past seven years trying to come to grips with the anger he'd felt for her, he would never have wanted her to endure what she'd had to go through.

He glanced around. She still sat on the sofa, her eyes downcast and her hands clasped in her lap. He'd thought she looked like a waif when she'd arrived. Now he realized she was a battered woman. Not only had Kyle hurt her physically, he had hurt her emotionally, and Lucas had no idea how to deal with it.

However, he did know how to deal with danger, and, from what Mia had told him, she was in a lot of danger right now. The one thing he still hadn't figured out was how Mia's caller had known she was at his house. If he hadn't followed her here, he had to have some way of keeping tabs on her. The answer hit him, and he groaned again.

"Of course. The car." He whirled around from the window and ran to the door. "I'll be right back," he called over his shoulder to a startled Mia.

Once outside he headed straight to Mia's car. It took only a few minutes to find the GPS tracker attached by a magnet to the inside fender of the back left tire. He pulled the tracker out, and an uneasy fear slowly curled through his body. When Mia had first begun to tell her story, he hadn't believed the threat to her to be that severe. Now, with Mia's account of the attack at her home, the threatening phone calls and a GPS tracker on her car, he knew it was serious. Deadly serious.

He stared down at the device in his hand before turning it off. Then he closed his fingers around it as he reentered the house. Mia stood just inside the front door, waiting for his return. When he walked in, her eyes grew wide. He motioned toward the living room. "Let's go back in there."

He followed her into the room and stopped

when she turned to face him. A puzzled expression flickered in her eyes. "Why did you go to my car?"

Lucas opened his hand. "To look for this."

She took one glance at what he held and frowned. "Wh-what is that thing?"

"It's a GPS device that was attached to your car. That's how your caller knew where you'd gone. As long as you kept using your car, he'd have known where you were at all times if I hadn't found it. I think we need to go to the police and tell them Chapman is stalking and threatening you."

"No!" A panicked look flashed across her face, and she glanced around as if in search of an escape route. "I can't go to the police. He said if I did, I'd end up with three bullet holes in my head."

Lucas reached out and grabbed her by the arm, pulling her to an abrupt stop. "We have to, Mia. My brother-in-law, Ryan Spencer, is a detective on the force. You don't have to go to the police station. I'll call him and have him come over here."

Mia tried to pull away from him. "I can't. I'm afraid," she cried out.

Lucas clamped his hands on her shoulders and stared down into her eyes. "I know you're afraid, and I understand. You've been through things in the past seven years that would have destroyed a weaker woman. But you're not weak, Mia. And you're not alone anymore. I'll help you face this."

She shook her head. "I'm not the same woman you once knew, Lucas. I can't do this. Maybe it's better if I just let Tony Chapman finish what Kyle tried to do many times—kill me."

A lock of hair had fallen across her forehead, and he reached up and gently smoothed it back into place. "You don't mean that."

She closed her eyes, and a tear ran down her cheek. "I do. I'm tired and scared, and I just want this to be over."

Lucas put his finger tip under her chin and tilted her face up. "Look at me, Mia." When she didn't respond, he nudged her again. "Please look at me."

Hesitantly, she opened her eyes and swallowed as she stared up into his face. "What?"

"Do you trust me?" he asked.

She gave a slight nod. "Yes."

"Then you need to do exactly as I say. I'm going to keep you safe from Tony Chapman, but we have to report this to the police. Now, I want you to sit back down on the couch while I call Ryan. When he arrives, you can tell him your story. Then we'll figure out where we go from here. Okay?"

After a moment she nodded, and he pulled his cell phone from his pocket and stepped back into the hallway to make the call. His brother-in-law answered right away. "Ryan," Lucas said, "I need to ask a favor of you."

"Sure. What is it?"

"I have a new client who's in trouble, and she needs to talk to the police but doesn't want to come to the station. Can you come over to my house?"

"I can. I'm on my way home now and can stop by, if that's okay."

"That's great. We'll see you soon."

He ended the call and walked back into the living room where Mia sat on the couch again. "Did you talk with Ryan?"

"I did. He's on his way. Would you like something to eat while we're waiting?"

She shook her head. "No. I just want to get this over with."

Lucas sat down beside her on the sofa. Mia shivered, and she reached for the afghan once more. "Are you cold?" Lucas asked. "Do I need to turn up the thermostat?"

"No. I think it's just nerves," she said as she wrapped the afghan around her.

There had to be some way to make her relax. He said the only thing he could think of. "Mia, I'm sorry I was curt with you earlier when you asked about my parents. They're doing well."

She turned her head toward him and smiled. "Really? That's good to know."

"In fact, they're doing great. Dad's enjoying retirement, but Mom still works part-time as a nurse. We all had dinner together at their house last night."

"All?"

"Yeah. Adam got married about a year and a half ago. His wife, Claire, works as the receptionist at the agency for us. They're expecting their first child in a few weeks. My sister, Jessica, married Ryan Spencer, the guy we're waiting for, about six months ago. She works with us, but she was Ryan's partner before she left the police force."

A smile tugged at the corner of Mia's lips. "That sounds like a wonderful family group." She hesitated a moment before she spoke again. "And what about you? Is there someone special in your life?"

Lucas chuckled and shook his head. "If you mean a woman, then the answer is no. If, on the other hand, you meant to say *something* special, then you must be referring to my motorcycle, and the answer is yes."

Her eyes crinkled at the corners the way he remembered as she giggled. "Oh, Lucas, you always could make me laugh."

The chiming of the doorbell sounded before he could reply, and he jumped to his feet. "That must be Ryan."

When he opened the front door, Ryan hurried into the house. "It's getting colder by the minute. I hope I don't get called out on a case tonight. I'm looking forward to spending a quiet night at home."

"I'd like to do that myself," Lucas said, "but I don't know about that at the moment."

Ryan cocked an eyebrow as he shrugged out of his coat. "You said you have a new client? What's going on?"

Lucas hesitated a few seconds as Ryan hung his coat on the hall tree. "It's kind of complicated," he said.

Ryan glanced toward the living room and then back to Lucas. "How?"

Lucas cleared his throat. "Has Jessica ever said anything to you about Mia Lockhart?"

Ryan nodded. "She's mentioned her. She was your girlfriend in college. Right?"

"Yeah. Well, she's in trouble, and I think the police need to know about it."

He led Ryan into the living room where Mia sat on the couch, her hands clasped in her lap. A worried expression covered her face, and her fingers trembled. She glanced from Ryan to Lucas as they entered. Ryan stepped over to the couch and held his hand out.

She reached up and shook his hand, and he settled on the couch next to her. "Mia, I'm Ryan Spencer, Lucas's brother-in-law. I'm a detective with the police department. Lucas said you're in trouble. Do you want to tell me about it?"

Her gaze darted to Lucas and then back to Ryan as she grasped the edge of the afghan and pulled it up to her neck. "Are you familiar with the Kyle Lockhart murder case?" she asked.

Ryan nodded. "I am. I know the detectives working the case against Tony Chapman. He must have some friends in high places if they were willing to post such a high bail. It didn't surprise us when he jumped bail."

"Kyle was my husband, but I never met Tony Chapman until after Kyle was killed," she said.

Lucas settled back and listened as Mia began to tell her story to Ryan, who made notes on a pad while she talked. From time to time he would ask a question, and she would respond. When she finished, Mia leaned back against the cushions of the sofa as if she was exhausted. Throughout her story, she hadn't mentioned anything about the abuse she had suffered from her husband. Maybe she thought the police already knew, since it was a matter of public record.

Ryan glanced over the notes he'd taken before he looked back at Mia. "And you have no idea what Chapman wants from you?"

"No." Her eyes grew wide, and the muscles in her throat rippled as she swallowed. "If I knew, I'd give it to him just to get rid of him. But I have no idea what it is."

Ryan flipped the notebook closed and inhaled. "It seems that he's determined to get whatever it is. Lucas did the right thing in getting you to talk to me. The police have been looking for Chapman, and we have some leads we're checking out. With Lucas on the case, too, hopefully it won't be long until he's caught. Until that time you need to be in a safe place. It doesn't sound like you should go home. Are there any family members you can stay with?"

Mia shook her head. "No. I told Lucas I could go to a hotel."

Ryan glanced at Lucas. "That's probably best. Maybe it will only take a few days for us to have him back in custody. Why don't you check into a hotel but stay in close touch with Lucas? We'll keep you posted on developments."

Lucas frowned. "Do you really think a hotel is a good idea?"

"There's nowhere else I can go, Lucas," Mia interrupted as she rose to her feet. "I've taken up too much of your time today. I'll find a hotel and let you know where I'm staying."

Lucas jumped to his feet, too, and shook his head. "No, I don't want you to go alone. I'll go with you and get you settled somewhere."

"Lucas, you don't have to—" she began.

"I think he should go with you, Mia," Ryan interrupted as he rose. "It's always better to be safe."

She shrugged. "Okay. If you think that's best."

Ryan turned to Lucas. "I'll check with you in the morning, but let me know if you need anything else tonight."

"I will," Lucas said as he ushered Ryan toward the door. "Tell Jessica I may be late getting to the office in the morning. I'll make sure Mia's okay before I come in."

"Will do."

Lucas closed the door behind Ryan and

turned back to the living room. Mia still stood in front of the couch, her hands clasped in front of her. Her lips trembled as a slight shiver rippled through her body. Lucas stopped in front of her and frowned. "Are you okay?"

She sucked in her breath and blinked. "Yeah, just tired. Except for my nap earlier, I haven't slept much in the last few days."

"Then let's get you to a hotel. You can order some room service and get settled for the night. I think we should leave your car here. If Chapman comes by to check on it after he realizes his tracker has been turned off, he'll see it and think you're still here."

"Okay." Her purse lay on the coffee table, and she reached for it just as a chime alerted her from the phone inside that a text had arrived. She looked up at him, a startled expression on her face, before she pulled the phone out. She stared down at the text, and then her body began to shake.

"What is it?" Lucas asked.

The phone slipped from her hand and dropped to the floor. Lucas reached down, picked it up and read the words of the message. I told you not to talk to the police.

Mia's hand clutched at her throat, and her

head shook from side to side in denial. "How does he know I talked to the police?"

"I don't know," Lucas muttered, "but he does. We need to get you out of here right away."

He grabbed her by the arm and pulled her toward the kitchen and out the door into the enclosed garage. Opening the back door of his car, he pushed Mia inside. "Lie down on the seat and don't sit up until we get to the hotel."

Then he jumped in the driver's seat, started the engine and raised the automatic garage door. As he backed out to the street, he scanned both ways in hopes of seeing a car where Chapman might be hiding, but he saw nothing unusual along either side of the street. A movement caught his eye as he shifted gears, and he glanced around to see the automatic garage door opening at the house of Mrs. Peterson, his elderly neighbor across the street. *Where could she be going at this time of day?* But sometimes when her daughter got off work, they met for dinner. She was probably headed to a restaurant right now to do that.

He dismissed the thought and turned his attention back to Mia, who lay in the backseat of his car. "Are you okay?" he asked.

"Yes."

"We'll be at the hotel in a few minutes." He

glanced in the rearview mirror once more as he turned the corner and pulled into the heavy afternoon traffic.

She didn't say anything, and he sighed as he rubbed his hand across his eyes. Hopefully, he was doing the right thing in putting Mia in a hotel. It didn't seem completely safe, but he didn't know what else he could do. This had certainly turned out to be the most surprising day he'd spent in a long time, and it had brought up too many memories he'd tried to ignore for years.

Maybe Chapman would be caught soon, and Mia could return home. Then he could put her out of his mind again and get on with the life he'd built for himself.

Fifteen minutes later Lucas unlocked the door to a room on the second floor of a midtown hotel and held it open for Mia to walk past him. She stopped just inside the door and turned to him. "Thank you, Lucas, for getting this room for me. I'll repay you."

He shook his head. "Don't worry about it. The agency will put it on your bill. For the time being, order your food from room service, and don't leave this room."

Her eyes blinked, and her breath hitched in

her throat. For a moment she had almost forgotten that this was a business arrangement. Of course Lucas wasn't helping her out of the kindness of his heart. She'd hired him to do a job for her, and this was just part of the services his agency supplied. His concern for her safety was no different than it would have been for any stranger who came to him for help.

She took a deep breath as a wobbly smile pulled at her lips. "I won't leave the room." She looked down at the jeans she'd been wearing since she left home. "Do you think it might be safe enough for me to go home tomorrow and get some clothes? If I'm going to be here for a while, I need to get some things."

He pursed his lips and frowned. "I don't know. We'll talk again tomorrow. For now, call the concierge downstairs, and he'll have anything you need sent up from the hotel's shop. You can charge those to the room, also."

"And you'll add them to my bill?"

His face flushed, but he nodded. "Yes."

She reached for the door handle and smiled again. "Thank you, Lucas, for all you've done for me today. I'll talk to you tomorrow."

A frown pulled at his brow. "Don't you want me to come in and check out your room?"

"There's no need in that. I'm sure it's fine."

He took a step back. "Then I'll see you in the morning. I'll come by before I go to the office."

Mia nodded. "I'll see you then."

Without waiting for him to reply, she closed the door and stood staring at it, her hands clenched to her side. Should she have asked him to come in? After all, he'd opened his home to her today and tried to make her feel safe.

After a moment she shook her head. Keeping her safe was his job. He'd already told her that their relationship would be purely business. She and Lucas had taken different paths, and they were no longer that young boy and girl who'd once loved each other. She'd seen to that, and she didn't think she would ever forgive herself for the choice she'd made.

With a sigh she walked over to the bed, sat down on the side and switched on the television with the remote. After a few minutes, she grew restless and wandered over to the window to look outside. The view of the parking lot behind the hotel left something to be desired.

Her stomach growled, reminding her that she hadn't eaten anything since Lucas had fixed her breakfast. She glanced at the desk in the room and spied a coffeepot. A cup of coffee and a sandwich was just what she needed. Once she had the coffee brewing, she called room service and sat down on the bed to flip through the channels to find something to watch. She'd just settled on a public television documentary when a knock sounded at the door. She glanced at her watch. No way could room service already be here.

She eased off the bed, tiptoed to the door, and leaned against it in hopes of hearing movement in the hall. When she heard nothing, she called out. "Who is it?"

"Maid service, ma'am. I need to put some clean towels in the bathroom," a man's voice called out.

Mia glanced at the closed door to the bathroom and frowned. She hadn't looked in there yet. Maybe the maids were behind schedule today and hadn't left towels earlier. She remembered seeing a man cleaning a room down the hall when she and Lucas had arrived earlier. Still, Lucas had told her to be careful before opening the door.

She took a deep breath. "Just leave them outside the door," she said.

"I can't do that, ma'am. The manager would fire me if he found out. I'll only be a minute. Quick in and out."

Mia reached for the doorknob and then pulled her hand away. She leaned forward and peered through the peephole into the hallway. A maid's cart piled high with clean towels and linens sat in front of her door. She couldn't see the man, but she caught a glimpse of his arm with towels draped over it. Underneath the towels she noticed a jacket like the one she'd seen on the hotel employee earlier.

She grasped the knob again and pulled the door open a few inches. "Okay, come on…"

Before she could finish her sentence, the door flew open, striking her in the chest with such a force that it knocked her backward where she landed like a sack of potatoes on the floor. Shaking her head to dispel her blurred vision, she scrambled backward as she stared up into the angry face of Tony Chapman. He slammed the door behind him and took a menacing step toward her.

"We meet again, Mrs. Lockhart," he snarled as he came nearer. "You went to the police after I warned you not to. I hope you remember what I told you."

Tears filled her eyes, and she shook her head. "Please, leave me alone. I've told you I don't know what you want."

A sinister smirk creased his mouth. "I think you do. Maybe you just need a reminder. Get up."

"P-please," she begged. "I don't know…"

"Get up! Don't make me kill you right here."

Mia pushed to her feet and held a hand out in front of her as she backed farther away from him. "You need to get out of here before I scream for help."

He laughed and took another step. "Scream and it'll be the last sound to come out of your mouth." He reached inside his jacket, pulled out a gun and aimed it at her. "Now do as I say. We're going to walk downstairs and out of this hotel. I will be right beside you with a gun in your ribs, and if you so much as raise an eyebrow to anybody, I'll kill you and whoever you try to alert. Do you understand?"

Mia's wide eyes stared down at the gun in Tony's hand, and she believed him. He wouldn't hesitate to kill her or anybody they came in contact with. She took a step backward and stopped as she bumped into the desk. "I'm not going with you."

"Oh, yes, you are."

She shook her head. "If I leave with you, I'll just be putting other people in danger. And if you kill me now, you'll never find out what you want to know. I can't very well tell you anything if I'm dead."

His eyes sparkled, and he took a step nearer. "So you do know where it is."

She lifted her chin and stared at him. "I didn't say that. But you don't know whether I do or not. If you kill me, you'll always wonder if I did."

An angry scowl covered his face, and he stormed toward her. "Tell me what you know right now, or I'm pulling this trigger."

He raised the gun, and she took a deep breath as she stared at the barrel pointed at her head. Taking another deep breath, she reached behind her, her fingers groping across the surface of the desk. He took one more step, and she clamped her fingers around the handle of the coffeepot.

"You're going to be sorry you messed with me," he muttered as he racked the first bullet into the semiautomatic gun's chamber.

"No, you're the one who's going to be sorry," she snarled.

Her hand whipped around as she hurled the scalding contents of the coffeepot at his face. A howl of pain rumbled from his throat, and his hands grabbed at his face. The gun tumbled to the floor.

Mia didn't hesitate but pushed past him and ran for the door. "Come back here!" he screamed as she ran into the hall.

The linen cart still sat outside her door, and she pushed it closer to the entrance to her room in hopes of delaying him. Behind her she could hear him yelling obscenities at her as he tried to follow.

She looked down the hall and decided her best avenue of escape was down the steps. She ran toward the stairs as fast as she could go. The sound of the door to her room crashing against the wall sent a wave of terror through her, but she didn't look back. At the end of the hall an exit sign above a door blinked its welcome to her, and she pushed through it like a speeding rocket. Her foot slipped as she hit the first step going down, and she stumbled, barely managing to grab the handrail.

Pain shot up her leg from her ankle, but she couldn't slow down. Escape was just a few feet away. Her heart dropped to the pit of her stomach when the door at the top of the stairs crashed open, and a man's footsteps echoed on the first steps.

She staggered down the last two steps and launched herself at the door leading into the lobby. The security officer near the hotel's front door looked around in surprise as she plowed into the room. She stumbled toward him.

"Help me!" she cried. "There's a man trying to kill me!"

The officer's eyebrows arched as he stared

past her. Before he could get his gun from the holster, a shot rang out, and he toppled to the floor. Mia glanced over her shoulder and screamed at the sight of Tony behind her, rage on his face evident under the red burn marks. He glared and pointed his gun at her.

Mia put up her hands and glanced around the lobby. Scared guests sat huddled in chairs and on the floor as they watched Tony stride closer to her. She backed away until she was beside the concierge's desk. His muffled voice drifted up from beneath the desk where he crouched on the floor. Her heartbeat quickened as she realized he was on the phone with the police.

Tony must have heard him, too, because he fired one shot at the desk. A groan followed by silence sent chills racing up Mia's spine. A woman across the lobby screamed, and Tony turned the gun in her direction.

Mia knew it was now or never. The front door was only a few feet away. If she ran, Tony might follow her and leave the others in the lobby alone. And she might be able to evade capture until the police arrived. She had only a split second to decide before he shot the woman who had yelled.

Breathing a quick prayer for God to watch over all of them, she turned and bolted for the front door.

FOUR

Lucas pocketed the receipt for the gasoline he'd just purchased, climbed back in the car and turned the key in the ignition. Good thing he'd noticed the gas gauge had been nearing empty when he left the hotel. He felt more comfortable knowing his vehicle was ready to go if he received an urgent call in the middle of the night.

He'd just put the car in gear when his cell phone rang. Ryan's name and number flashed on the caller ID on the vehicle's dashboard screen. With a frown he connected the call.

"Hey, Ryan. What's up?"

"Where are you, Lucas?"

Lucas stiffened at the curt tone. "I left Mia at the hotel, and now I'm headed home. I stopped for gas. Why?"

"Because I'm at the house of Mrs. Peterson, who lives across the street from you. Her daughter came home from work and found her mother tied to a chair in the living room. She's been held prisoner in her home all day by a man who's been watching your house from her front window."

"What?" Lucas shouted.

"Yeah, he stole her car and left nearly an hour ago. The EMTs are getting ready to take her to the hospital, but I pulled up Tony Chapman's picture on my cell phone. She identified him as the man."

Lucas's stomach clenched. This explained how Chapman knew Ryan had come to his house. The memory of seeing Mrs. Peterson's car pulling out of her garage flashed into Lucas's mind, and he sucked in his breath. How could he have dismissed what he'd seen without checking on it? He hadn't even looked to see if Mrs. Peterson's car had followed him to the hotel. He had to get to Mia right away. But he might already be too late. If his negligence had caused anything to happen to her, he would never forgive himself.

"I'm heading back to the hotel," he yelled as he floored the accelerator and did a quick turn onto the street from where he had just come.

Swerving in and out of traffic, his hand pressed to the car's horn and his caution lights blinking, he drove like a madman toward the hotel. Behind him he could hear sirens. The police had to be after him for speeding. Good. He increased his speed. Now to lead them right to the hotel.

He roared into the hotel driveway and screeched to a stop at the front door. He was out of the car by the time the engine died. Suddenly the front door of the hotel swung open, and Mia ran outside, her face a mask of terror.

Her eyes grew wide when she saw him. "Lucas!" she screamed. "Tony Chapman's after me."

He reached her in two steps, grabbed her by the arm and propelled her behind him. He held her with one arm protectively as he shielded her with his body and pulled his gun from its holster with his other hand. Behind him three police cars and two ambulances came to a halt, and suddenly officers swarmed around them.

"Where is the shooter, ma'am?" one of the men asked.

Mia raised a shaking hand and pointed toward the hotel entrance. "Inside."

Lucas glanced at the door, and the image of a man holding a gun was visible through the glass. A surprised look flashed on his face before he turned and disappeared from sight.

Mia had seen the same thing. "That's him!" she screamed.

The police officers fanned out, some going around the side of the hotel and others toward the door. As they moved forward, their guns drawn, Lucas pulled Mia back toward his car. Two EMTs jumped from each of the ambulances, and the four crouched low as they followed the lawmen to the door. Evidently they expected a large number of injuries and had come prepared. Within minutes all of them disappeared into the building.

Lucas pulled Mia around to the far side of his car, using the vehicle as somewhat of a shield for them. He stopped beside the car's back door, shoved his gun in its holster and grasped her by both arms. "Are you okay?"

She nodded, and then it was as if the fight went out of her body. She sagged and would have dropped to the ground if he hadn't been holding her. His grip on her tightened, and he pulled her to him. She clutched his jacket with both hands and buried her face in his chest as she sobbed. He wrapped one arm around her waist and held her as his other hand stroked the back of her head. She'd taken her hair down from its earlier ponytail, and the strands felt like silk slipping through his fingers. He swallowed at the memory that hit him in the pit of his stomach, but he couldn't pull his hand away.

"Don't cry," he whispered. "It's over now. The police will catch him."

"H-he shot two people inside, and he was going to kill me."

A shiver went through her, and her fingers tightened on his coat. After a moment she quieted, and he loosened his hold on her. "Tell me what happened."

She took a deep breath and pulled away. Another tear trickled from her eye, and she swiped at it with her fingers. "I shouldn't have opened the door," she said.

He listened as she told him what had transpired in her room after he had left. When she'd finished, he shook his head in regret. "I shouldn't have brought you here and left you alone. I'm sorry."

"It wasn't your fault. I didn't think it would be so easy for him to find me."

Lucas exhaled. "I'm afraid that's my fault, too."

Her eyes grew wide as he related what Ryan had told him on the phone. "So, I made a mistake, and you almost died because of it," he said. "I'm so sorry, Mia, but I promise you it won't happen again. I'm going to protect you until this guy is caught."

At that moment the hotel door opened, and one of the policemen walked outside. Mia straightened her shoulders and took a deep breath. "Maybe they already have captured him."

Lucas recognized Matt Devlin, the officer walking toward him. He'd met him several times at the precinct when Lucas had been returning a fugitive to custody. It wasn't difficult to tell from Matt's somber expression that he didn't have good news for them.

Matt stopped in front of them and shook his head. "Looks like he gave us the slip. The officers that circled to the back of the hotel saw him run out the rear entrance as they were coming around the corner of the building. They chased him for two blocks before he circled back around, jumped in a car and took off. They got the license plate and notified dispatch, but no one has spotted the car yet."

"Probably my neighbor's car. He'll ditch it and steal another one soon."

Mia glanced at the hotel entrance and then back to Matt. "What about the security officer and the concierge that Tony shot? How are they?"

Matt's forehead wrinkled. "The security

officer has lost a lot of blood. The EMTs are trying to get him stabilized so they can transport him. The concierge has a flesh wound in the shoulder and should be okay. If he hadn't taken the chance on making the call to 911, Chapman might have shot a lot more people. He's the hero today."

Mia swallowed, and her eyes filled with tears. "May I see him?"

Matt nodded. "They'll be out with him in a minute. You should be able to speak to him then." He turned toward Lucas and fixed him with a steady gaze. "What's your connection to this, Knight?"

"Mrs. Lockhart hired me to find Tony Chapman since he jumped bail and has been threatening her. I thought this hotel would be a safe place for her to stay, but I seem to have been wrong."

Matt chuckled. "Yeah, I guess you could say that." He glanced back at the entrance and then to Mia. "I have to get back inside, but I'll need to take your statement before you leave."

Lucas nodded. "We'll wait for you."

Matt nodded and turned back to the front doors just as they opened. Two of the EMTs emerged pushing a gurney bearing the concierge. Pain etched his pale face, and he bit down on his lip. Mia ran forward and met the stretcher as they approached the waiting ambulance. She grasped his hand.

"Thank you so much for making that call," she said. "You saved the lives of many people today."

A wan smile pulled at his lips. "It's all part of the job, ma'am. We try to keep our guests safe."

"Well, you certainly kept me safe, and I'll never forget you."

He smiled, and then the EMTs hoisted the gurney into the back of the ambulance and shut the door. Lucas stepped up beside Mia and watched as the vehicle pulled out into traffic, its lights flashing.

Mia exhaled a long breath and turned to stare at Lucas. "I want you to know I've learned my lesson. Next time I won't open the door to my room."

"What do you mean?"

She gave a short chuckle. "I mean that next time I'll call down to the desk and make sure someone from the hotel has come to my room."

Lucas shook his head. "There's not going to be a next time. You're not staying here now that Chapman knows where you are."

She frowned and tilted her head to one side.

"Then do you have another hotel in mind where I can stay?"

He nodded. "I have the perfect place, and I'm taking you there now."

"Where is it?"

"My parents' house. You're going to be their guest until Tony Chapman is caught."

"But I can't go to your parents' home," Mia argued for perhaps the tenth time.

Lucas, who so far had concentrated on driving and appearing deaf to her objections, finally released a long breath and glanced her way. "Knock it off, Mia. You're going, and that's all there is to it."

"But I haven't seen them in years, and I'm sure they hate me because of how things ended with us."

A muscle in Lucas's jaw flexed, and his mouth tightened into a grim line. "They don't hate you. My parents don't hold grudges."

Mia crossed her arms, leaned back and stared out the window at the streetlights as Lucas's car sped along the Memphis streets. Her stomach roiled at the thought of having to see Lucas's parents after all this time. How could she face them after she'd treated their son so badly seven years ago?

"Have you told your mother you're bringing me there?"

"No. I called, but her phone went to voice mail. I figured they might have gone out to dinner."

She stared at him. "So, you're going to show up at their door after all these years with me in tow and expect them to unfurl the red carpet? I don't think so."

Lucas glanced at her and rolled his eyes. "Don't worry about it, Mia. My parents are committed to doing whatever they can to help clients of the Knight Agency."

"Even if that client is someone who hurt their son in the past?"

Lucas narrowed his eyes. "Like you said, that's in the past. It has nothing to do with this case. Now, don't worry about it anymore."

Mia started to protest, but she knew it would do no good. She stared at him for a moment before she cleared her throat and took a deep breath. "You're sure I won't make them uncomfortable?"

"I'm sure. They're remarkable people, even if they are my parents. When I was going through such a rough time after you broke up with me, they would always tell me that I needed to pray for you. My mother would say that we often don't like things that people do, but we can still like the person that they are. She encouraged me to pray for you, and I did."

Her eyes filled with tears. "You did?"

"Yeah. I didn't know where you were or what you were doing. But I would pray that God would watch over you. I prayed that even on the days I was the angriest with you, and that's what finally saved me. One day I realized there was no need to hate you anymore. Of course if I had known what you were going through, I might have prayed harder."

She stared off into space a few seconds before she turned to him and smiled. "Maybe it was those prayers that protected me when I thought nothing could. Thank you, Lucas."

He reached over and took her hand in his. "I'm sorry I forgot that when you appeared on my doorstep. At the first sight of you I'm afraid all my old feelings came back, but I have them under control now. If I'm going to help you, we need to be friends. So let's put the past behind us and live in the present. There's a killer out there who needs to be caught."

Her vision blurred with unshed tears, and she smiled. "That sounds good. Thank you, Lucas."

He didn't say anything for a moment. Then he cleared his throat and smiled. "What do you say to getting something to eat before I take you to my parents' house? I promise I'll keep a better lookout for someone following us this time. I won't let anything happen to you again."

She only hoped that no harm came to him or his family because of the trouble she'd brought here. The thought that she might be the cause of misfortune for them was even more worrying than the thought of Tony Chapman making good on his threat to put three bullet holes in her head.

Lucas drained the last drop from his coffee cup and set it back in the saucer as he let his gaze drift over the other customers in the restaurant. He'd chosen this place because it was blocks away from the hotel where Mia had encountered Tony Chapman. He'd taken a circuitous route getting there and had kept a close watch for any car that might be following, but he'd seen nothing out of the ordinary.

Across from him, Mia slid the last bite of pecan pie into her mouth and reached for her coffee cup. She'd raised it a few inches when it suddenly slipped from her hand and clattered to the saucer. Before he could say anything she grabbed her napkin and swabbed at the stain on the white tablecloth.

A waitress appeared at the side of the table, a dish towel in her hand, and smiled down at Mia. "Let me help you with that."

Mia's face flushed as she stared up at the young woman and then back to Lucas. "I'm sorry."

The waitress shook her head. "No problem. We have accidents like this all the time." She finished soaking up the stain and set Mia's cup upright in the saucer. "Would you like some more coffee?"

Mia shook her head. "No, but thank you for your help."

The woman smiled again before heading toward the kitchen. When she'd disappeared inside, Mia folded her hands in her lap and stared down at them. "I'm sorry to be so clumsy, Lucas. I'll be more careful next time."

Something in the tone of her voice made Lucas's stomach twist, and he almost gasped aloud. The expression on Mia's face reminded him of a penitent child, one who was awaiting some harsh punishment. Mia might be away from Kyle, but apparently she was still paying the price of what he'd done to her emotionally.

After a moment he clasped his hands in front of him on the table and leaned closer. "Mia," he said softly, "it's okay. No big deal. Just some spilled coffee. No one's angry with you."

She didn't look up right away, but when she did, his heart pricked at the fear in her eyes. "Old habits die hard, Lucas. If this had happened at home with Kyle, I would be lying on the floor with blood pouring from my nose right now."

Lucas swallowed the bile that rushed into his mouth and tried to smile. "Well, you're not at home, and Kyle is never going to hurt you again. In fact, we need to get going so I can get you to my parents' home."

Her gaze drifted over his face for a moment before a weak smile pulled at her lips. "Thank you for being so nice to me, Lucas. But I should have known you would be. You always were a wonderful person, and I treated you so badly. I have regretted that more than you'll ever know." She took a deep breath and straightened her back. "But I want you to know that you don't have anything to fear from me. I haven't come back into your life expecting that we can regain what we once had. I think we both know that isn't possible. We're different people now than we were then."

"I'm glad you see it that way, Mia. It makes it easier for me to work for you."

She nodded. "I realize you have your own life, and I don't want to cause you any problems. I also don't want to cause any problems for your parents or put them in danger by staying in their home. Tony has already found me at your house and at the hotel. What if he tracks me to your parents' home?"

Lucas shook his head and chuckled. "You're forgetting what business we're in. We're all well trained in firearms and defense techniques. My mother is as tough as they come, and my father can still take down my brother and me. My brother-in-law is a police detective. I'd say you have some of the best bodyguards around."

She laughed, and he heard a bit of relief in the sound. "Okay. If you say so. Now I'm going to the ladies' room before we leave."

He smiled and pulled his cell phone from his pocket. "Good. I'll try to call Mom again to tell her I'm bringing you over."

Lucas watched until she'd stepped away before he punched his mother's cell phone number into the phone. She answered right away.

"Hello, youngest son. How are you today?"

Lucas smiled at the love that always filtered through her words. He especially liked it when she called him youngest son. For some reason it made him feel special.

"I'm good, Mom. I have a favor to ask you."

"Uh-oh," she said. "Is that motorcycle broken down again and you need a loan?"

He chuckled. "As if you'd ever spend a dime on my bike. But, no, it's not for me, and it's not about money. It's about a new client. She's in a bit of a jam. Her husband was murdered, and the accused killer jumped bail. Now he's threatening her, and she hired me to bring him in. She can't stay at home because he knows where she lives, and he's already attacked her there. I tried to put her up in a hotel, but he found her there, too. She needs a safe place to stay for a few days. Are you up to having a houseguest?"

His mother didn't hesitate. "Of course. Bring her on over. I can put her in Jessica's old room."

"Thanks, Mom." He bit down on his lip before he continued. "There's just one thing. This client is Mia."

His mother didn't say anything for a moment, but he heard her sharp intake of breath. "Mia Fletcher?"

"Yeah. Only she's Mia Lockhart now."

"Lucas, are you sure about taking this case on? You know what a hard time you had getting over her."

"I know, Mom. But she's in bad trouble. She needs somebody like you to make her feel safe.

She's never had anybody who loved her enough to protect her."

"Except you," his mother said in a voice so low it made every nerve ending in his body scream.

"Except me. But that was a long time ago, and I won't go back there. She's had a rough time." He swallowed and tightened his grip on the phone as the memory of how Mia had looked minutes ago flashed in his mind. "Mom, not only is the guy who killed her husband after her, but she's been a victim of some really bad domestic abuse for years. I just want to help her."

"Very well, then. This is the place for her. Bring her on, and we'll do everything we can. But be careful, Lucas. I love you and don't want to see you hurt again."

"I love you, too, Mom. We'll be there in a little while."

Lucas disconnected the call and slipped the phone back in his pocket. Twenty-four hours ago he would never have believed that he would be having dinner with Mia and that he would be making plans to have her stay with his parents while he tried to track down her husband's killer. But then, in his profession, he was used to sudden surprises. He was a bounty hunter with an appetite for living free and doing what he liked. That was what he'd decided he wanted years ago, and he wasn't about to lose control of the life he'd carved out for himself. That wasn't going to change because Mia had walked back into his life.

Mia was just a client. Nothing more. He would do everything in his power to find Tony Chapman. When he did have him back in custody and the case was over, he was going to walk away and not look back.

And Mia Fletcher Lockhart could go wherever she wanted, as long as it was far, far away from him.

FIVE

When Lucas stopped his car in the driveway of his parents' home, a momentary flash of panic rippled through Mia's body. Lucas had assured her his mother wanted her to come, but she still found it hard to believe. How could the Knight family welcome her into their home after the way she had hurt their son?

Beside her Lucas turned off the ignition and glanced at her. "Here we are. Ready to go inside?"

She stared out the window at the two-story brick home that sat in the cul-de-sac of an upscale neighborhood and sucked in her breath at the sight. Christmas lights beamed in a blaze of glory along the rooflines, windows and porches of every home up and down the street, and Mia felt as if she'd stepped into a Christmas winter wonderland.

Her gaze shifted to the door on the Knights'

front porch, where an evergreen wreath glittered with huge red bows and red berries. The glimmer of electric candles sitting in the windows cast a glow across the porch, but it was the lights from a Christmas tree inside one of the rooms to the right of the door that took her breath away.

"I really hadn't realized that it's getting so close to Christmas," she whispered.

Lucas chuckled. "How could you ignore all the holiday shopping advertising on TV and in stores?"

She shook her head. "I guess Tony Chapman is the only thing I've been able to think about for weeks." Her brow wrinkled, and she looked at Lucas. "But you know my father and I never celebrated Christmas. He thought it was a waste of time, and so did Kyle."

Lucas smiled. "Then you'd better get ready for a rude awakening. The Knight family goes all out for holidays. And with Christmas a little over a week away, my mom is on a mission to make this the best one ever. This year we're thankful to have two new additions to our family—Ryan, in addition to Adam and Claire's expected baby."

His words pricked at her heart, and she thought about what it would be like to celebrate

Christmas with a family. The memory of visiting the Knights in happier times assaulted her, and she blinked back tears. She remembered Lucas's twin sister, Jessica, and his brother, Adam, and wondered how they would feel having her back in their lives—even if it was only for a short time.

She tried to smile, but her mouth seemed to wobble. "Maybe it won't matter. I should be gone from here before Christmas anyway."

He pressed his lips together and opened the door, hopped out and came around to the passenger side of the car. Before Mia could grasp the handle, Lucas had pulled the door open and stood smiling down at her. She inhaled a quick breath and glanced up at him, her pulse pounding. It had been a long time since a man had offered her such a courtesy. All Kyle had ever done was berate her for not getting out of the car fast enough. It felt so good for a man to show her this small bit of respect, and she was glad it was Lucas.

Still smiling, she climbed from the vehicle and followed him up the stone walkway to the entrance to the house. As if those inside were watching for their arrival, the door swung open before they stepped on the front porch. Lucas's mother stood in the doorway, a warm smile on her lips.

"Come on in," she said as she pulled the door open wider. "We've been waiting for you."

Mia stepped into the house and inhaled. "What is that amazing scent?" she asked.

Mrs. Knight smiled as she closed the door. "That's some cinnamon spice potpourri I have simmering. I think it gives the house a festive aroma."

"It's wonderful," Mia said.

Lucas laughed. "One of Mom's old recipes and one of my favorites. Christmas wouldn't seem the same without that smell in the house."

Mia glanced at Mrs. Knight, who was staring at her son with a slight smile on her face, her love for him evident in the way her eyes caressed his features. Did Lucas realize how lucky he was to have someone love him like that?

Mia cleared her throat. "Mrs. Knight, I want to thank you for opening your home to me. I know it's an imposition, especially at this time of year, but I do appreciate it."

Mrs. Knight pulled her gaze away from Lucas and smiled at Mia. Then she stepped closer, put her arms around Mia's shoulders and drew her into an embrace. "Mia, it is no imposition at all. We're glad to have you."

A loud crash accompanied by a man's voice rang out from the back of the house. "No problem! I just knocked a chair over. No damage done."

Lucas and his mother both laughed, and Lucas arched his eyebrows as he stared at his mother. "It sounds like Dad's back in the kitchen again. I thought you had put it off-limits for him."

His mother shook her head in despair. "He wanted to make some cocoa for us to have with my fresh batch of oatmeal cookies when Mia got here. Let's check on him."

Mia followed Mrs. Knight into the kitchen. As she walked through the door, she remembered happier times when she had visited here with Lucas. Back then, she had thought this room seemed to be the heart of the household, and it still gave off that same feeling.

Mr. Knight came around the table when they entered and stopped next to Mia. He took her hand in his and stared into her eyes. "Welcome to our home, Mia. Lucas tells us you're having a rough time right now. We're glad you've come to us for help. And, please, know you're welcome to stay as long as you need to."

Mia stared up into eyes so like Lucas's and blinked back tears. These people should hate her. Instead they had opened their home and welcomed her as if she was an honored guest. It had been so long since anyone treated her with kindness that she hardly knew how to respond.

"Th-thank you," she finally stammered.

Mr. Knight pulled out a chair. "Have a seat, and I'll pour you a cup of cocoa."

Mia sank down in the chair and smiled as Lucas and his parents settled at the table. A comfortable feeling spread through her as she listened to them discuss their plans for the upcoming Christmas dinner. She wrapped her hands around her cup and relaxed back in her chair, watching the way Lucas's face beamed with happiness at the lively conversation.

It was good to see him laugh and enjoy himself. In the years they'd been apart, she had often wondered what his life was like, and now she was getting to see for herself. The hypnotic lull of the voices around her combined with the marshmallow-topped hot chocolate drifted over her like a warm blanket, and she found herself almost nodding off to sleep.

A chime from her cell phone startled her, and she jerked up straight in her chair. Before she had time to consider what she was doing, she had pulled the phone from her pocket.

Lucas jumped to his feet and pushed his chair backward. "Mia, don't read that."

But it was too late. She'd already opened the text message, and all she could do was stare in horror at what she saw.

A photo of Tony Chapman's profile filled the screen. Mia gasped and covered her mouth with her free hand at the sight of the red blistering welts that streaked his face. As gruesome as the picture was, though, it was the words across the bottom of the text that sucked the breath from her throat.

You're going to pay for this. Can't wait to hear you beg for mercy.

Lucas charged around the table and jerked the phone from Mia's hands. His eyebrows shot up as he saw the picture and read the message. Mia cringed in her chair, her fists clutched in her lap, and stared up at him with a panic-filled expression in her eyes. His heart lurched. He'd failed again and let Chapman get to her.

He glanced at his parents, whose shocked faces gaped at him. "What is it?" his mother asked.

"Mia threw a pot of coffee in Chapman's face

when he came after her at the hotel. He sent her a picture of the burns."

His mother held out her hand. "May I see the picture?"

Lucas nodded at her mother. The tone of her voice told him she had gone into nurse mode. "Sure. Look at this and give me your diagnosis."

She studied the photo for a few moments before she glanced up. "Definitely second-degree burns. Were the police going to contact the emergency rooms?"

Lucas shrugged. "I don't know. I'll call Ryan and ask him."

His mother looked back at the picture. "These burns may not be bad enough to leave scarring, but they have to be very painful." Her mouth pulled into a big grin as she handed the phone back to Lucas. "Mia, I have to hand it to you. That took some fast thinking."

Lucas crouched down beside Mia's chair and covered her hands with his. "It did, but I'm sorry it happened. I should have told you to turn your cell phone off, so he couldn't harass you anymore. But you have to realize, Chapman is playing with your head right now. He wants to frighten you so you'll make a mistake."

She stared down at his hand covering hers.

His thumb gently brushed across the top of her hand, and she didn't move for a moment. Then she looked up at him, and a slight smile curled the corners of her lips. "I-if h-he's trying to frighten me, he's doing a good job."

Lucas chuckled and squeezed her hand once more before he released her. "He only wins if you let him. We'll get through this, but you have to be strong. Don't start doubting yourself. We can't let him think he has the upper hand."

"I don't feel very strong at the moment."

Lucas glanced at his parents. "And this from the woman who has already gotten the upper hand with Chapman twice. Once she sprayed him with pepper spray, and the second time she threw hot coffee in his face."

Mr. Knight shook his head and laughed. "With skills like that, Mia, you may have the makings of a bounty hunter."

Mia's face flushed as she glanced around the table. "Thank you, but I don't think that's going to happen. I'm not a very brave person. All of you, on the other hand, are the opposite."

Lucas took a deep breath. "You have it in you to be brave, too."

Mia waved her hand in dismissal. "What makes you think that?"

"Do you remember when we were in college,

and you got sick with the flu the week before you were to dance the role of the Sugar Plum Fairy in *The Nutcracker*?"

The muscles in her throat constricted as she swallowed. "Of course I remember."

"And your understudy was bragging all over campus that she was going to get to dance the role since you were sick."

A soft giggle bubbled up out of Mia's throat. "Her name was Cindy Gray. She was really upset when I won out over her."

Lucas chuckled. "Yeah, I remember. After all, the Sugar Plum Fairy is the most sought-after role in the whole ballet."

Mia closed her eyes for a moment. "I was so sick the week before the performance, and I didn't think I could do it."

Lucas took her hand in his. "But you did. That's the point I'm trying to make. You came to the theater, and you went out on that stage and danced better than you ever had in rehearsal."

Tears filled Mia's eyes. "I did, didn't I?"

"And you did it because you were determined not to let anything stop you from dancing that night. I was there, Mia, and it was a stunning performance. You even got a standing ovation."

"Yes, I did," she whispered. "But, what's your point, Lucas?"

"My point is that you didn't give in to fear or doubt that night. You reached down inside yourself and found the courage and strength that you needed to get you through that performance. You've had some bad things happen to you since then, but I believe that girl I once knew is inside you somewhere. I want you to reach down and find the drive that's going to get you through this ordeal with Tony Chapman. We're going to catch him. But until we do, I need you to be strong. Can you do that?"

She thought for a moment before she slowly nodded. "I can."

Lucas smiled and pushed to his feet. "Good. Now I want you to give me that cell phone. Tomorrow I'll get you a burner phone that you can use while I'm looking for Chapman." He held up her phone before slipping it in his pocket. "Then, when this is over, I'll give the phone back to you."

Her lips trembled as she smiled. "Thanks, Lucas. I knew I'd come to the right person to help me."

Before he could answer, his mother pushed to her feet. "Mia, you look exhausted. Let me show you to your room, and you can take a shower and get in bed."

"Oh, that sounds good," she said as she rose and glanced around the table. "Good night, and thank you again."

She started for the door but turned and glanced back at Lucas. "When will I see you next?"

"I'll come by in the morning."

"Do you think I might be able to go home and get some clothes?"

"We'll talk about it then," he said.

She nodded and followed his mother from the room. Within seconds he heard the clatter of them climbing the stairs. He turned back to his father, who was regarding him quizzically. "Are you okay, son?" he asked.

Lucas frowned and nodded. "Yes. Why wouldn't I be?"

His father sighed and shrugged. "I just wondered how you felt about seeing Mia after all these years."

That was a good question, and one he didn't have an answer to. Finally he said the only thing he could think of. "I'm okay. She's just a client."

His father studied him for a moment, before he nodded and stood. "I need to check the Christmas lights outside. I'll see you before you leave."

Lucas sat back down in his chair and wrapped his hands around his cup. He didn't say anything as his father walked from the room. Tangled thoughts raced through his head.

Mia as the Sugar Plum Fairy. Mia telling him she wasn't going to marry him. Mia appearing on his doorstep. Mia's battered face staring at him from his computer screen. He closed his eyes and squeezed the cup harder.

"Are you okay?"

His mother's voice startled him, and his eyes flew open. He straightened in his chair and tried to smile. "Dad asked that, too, but I'm just tired. I'd better get on home."

His mother's eyes narrowed, and a slight frown pulled at her brow. "Lucas, be careful."

He let out a short chuckle as he stood. "I will be, Mom. I've handled guys like Tony Chapman lots of times. I'll watch my step."

She stepped up beside him and cupped his jaw in her hand. "I'm talking about Mia. Be careful. She's vulnerable right now, and she needs someone. Just guard against anything that's going to bring you more heartache."

He could see love for him shining in his mother's eyes, and he leaned forward and kissed her cheek. "I will, Mom. And thanks for worrying about me."

"I pray for you every day, Lucas. That's what keeps me from worrying about you, but that doesn't mean I don't care what happens to you. I do."

"I know you do." He took a deep breath. "Now I need to get out of here. I'll come by tomorrow morning at nine o'clock to check on Mia."

He started to walk toward the door, but his mother grabbed his arm and stopped him. "Oh, I nearly forgot to tell you. I'm working at the hospital tomorrow, and your dad is going into the office to help Claire with some end-of-the-year accounting. What should we do about Mia? I don't think she needs to be alone."

Lucas raked his hand through his hair and grimaced. "No, she doesn't. I'm going to do some checking on Chapman. I guess she can come with me."

"Are you sure?"

Lucas shrugged. "I don't know what else I can do. She can't stay alone." He gave his mother another quick kiss and then headed to his car. His dad was in the front yard adjusting some lights when he walked outside, and he waved to him before he got in his vehicle and drove away.

When he arrived home, he noticed Mrs. Peterson's house across the street lit up and the porch light on. Maybe she hadn't had to stay at the hospital. He parked in his garage and walked over. Mrs. Peterson's daughter, Julie, answered the door.

"Lucas, come in."

He stepped inside and glanced around. Although he and Mrs. Peterson often talked when they were out in the yard, he'd been in her home only one or two times. He stopped in the entry and turned around as Julie closed the door.

"My brother-in-law was one of the policemen who came today, and he called me to tell me what happened. I wanted to come by and see your mother and tell her how sorry I am for what she had to endure."

Julie smiled and him forward. "She's doing well. The doctor didn't think she needed to stay overnight at the hospital. She wasn't injured, just dehydrated, and we're taking care of that. Come on in the den. She's in there."

Lucas followed Julie down the hall and into a room where Mrs. Peterson was propped up on a plump sofa, watching a reality show on a big-screen TV. A roaring fire crackled in the fireplace.

She sat up straight and held out her hand when Lucas came in. "Lucas, how good to see you."

He grasped her hand in both of his and leaned closer to her. "I can't tell you how sorry I am for what you suffered today. I brought this trouble to your door, and I'm so sorry."

Mrs. Peterson smiled and motioned him to a chair. "When I identified the picture of the man who'd held me captive, the police told me he was an accused killer who'd jumped bail and that you'd been hired to track him down."

"Yes, but you should never have been involved. I'm so sorry."

She thought for a moment before she spoke. "I admit it was scary. He kept waving a gun in front of my face and telling me if I made a sound he'd shoot me, but he was really focused on keeping an eye on your house."

"I know. The person who hired me spent the day at my house. She's been terrorized by Chapman for weeks ever since he murdered her husband. She came to me because she didn't feel safe in her home, but he tracked her to my house and watched to see where she was going next." Lucas scooted to the edge of his seat and clasped his hands between his knees. "Did he say anything out of the ordinary while he was here?"

Mrs. Peterson frowned. "Like what?"

Lucas spread his hands and shrugged. "Like where he might be going next? Anything."

Mrs. Peterson thought for a moment before she shook her head. "Nothing like that. He did make some phone calls."

"Do you know who to?"

She shook her head. "He didn't tell me. One of them I assumed was his sister. He kept calling her Sis, and once when he got angry at something she'd said, he said her name, which was Nadine. Then he talked to someone else. I don't know whether it was a man or a woman, but he said something about how he was going to find that missing shipment if it was the last thing he ever did."

"But he didn't say what the shipment was or why it was missing?"

"No. And that's all I remember. Except one thing." She closed her eyes and bit down on her lip.

Lucas leaned forward. "What was that?"

She opened her eyes, and they sparkled with tears. "He was looking out the window, and suddenly he jumped to his feet and demanded to know where I kept my car keys. I told him, and he said he was going to borrow my car. I had a moment of relief that he was finally going. But then, he…"

Lucas reached for her hand as she struggled to speak. "Then what?"

Mrs. Peterson took a deep breath. "Then he stepped closer and pointed his gun at me. He had an evil expression on his face, and he slowly raised his gun and pointed it at me. He said, 'I need to do one more thing before I go.' I began to cry and beg him not to kill me. But he just laughed, and then after a few moments he pulled the trigger, and it clicked on an empty chamber. He laughed louder and said 'Bang!' Without another word he turned and ran outside."

Lucas squeezed the woman's hands as she began to shake. "I'm so sorry."

She looked up and smiled through her tears. "It's not your fault, Lucas. I knew he was a terrible person the minute I laid eyes on him. He terrorized me all day, and then he nearly gave me a heart attack at the end when I thought he was going to kill me. But I'm okay. Now you have to find him and make sure he faces justice for everything he's done."

He swallowed hard and nodded. "I will, Mrs. Peterson."

Her eyes raked his face as she clasped his hands in hers. "Your parents raised a good man, Lucas. You've been so kind to me. You mow my yard in the summer, and you take my garbage cans to the street every week and put them up again. I don't know what I would do without you."

His throat clogged with emotion as he squeezed her hands before releasing her and pushing to his feet. "I'm glad to help any way I can. And the next thing I have to do for you is find Tony Chapman and get him back in jail."

"Be careful."

"I will. Now you rest and get your strength back." He glanced at Julie. "Are you staying with her tonight?"

She nodded. "I am."

He let out a sigh of relief. "Good. I didn't like the idea of her being alone."

Julie led him back to the front door, and he walked across the street to his place. When he entered the dark house, he was suddenly aware of how silent it was. Usually he welcomed coming home to the peace and solitude, but tonight another feeling drifted through the rooms.

He stood in the kitchen for a moment trying

to figure out what it was. At first he thought it must have been a reaction to the events of the day, but it went deeper than that. Then it hit him. The house felt empty. Just like his life. He could tell his parents and friends that he had the kind of life he wanted—that he had no desire to clutter up his life with things like a wife and kids and responsibilities. But it wasn't true. He was lonely.

He ambled back into the living room, sat down on the couch where Mia had lain all day and picked up the afghan he'd covered her with. The scent of her perfume drifted to his nose, and he closed his eyes as he inhaled.

After a moment he laid the afghan aside and pulled out his cell phone. Ryan answered on the first ring. "Hey, Lucas. What's up?"

"I have a question, Ryan. Do you know if Tony Chapman has a sister named Nadine?"

"Yeah, he does. Her name is Nadine McElroy. She lives in a neighborhood off Perkins Street. I don't know the street or the number."

"That's okay. I can find that out."

"What do you want to know about her?"

"I need to ask her some questions about her brother. Maybe she knows where he is."

"Well, good luck getting her to tell you anything." Ryan paused a moment before he spoke again. "I heard about what happened at the hotel. It sounds like your client is some kind of woman. Good thing she had that pot of coffee handy."

Lucas laughed. "Yeah. She's been amazing today." He took a deep breath. "I didn't let her stay at the hotel, though. I took her to Mom and Dad's house."

Ryan didn't say anything for a moment. "Sounds like the best place for her."

"I thought so, too. Well, I have to go. I'll talk to you tomorrow."

He hung up, walked to the window and stared at Mrs. Peterson's house across the street. His heart lurched at the thought of how close Mia and Mrs. Peterson had come to being killed today. If either one of them had died, it would have been his fault.

Gritting his teeth, he pulled Mia's phone from his pocket and stared at the last text Chapman had sent her. He didn't know if Chapman's phone would receive his message, but he hoped it would. He had one for him.

Lucas began to type, and when he was finished, he read what he had written. Your time is running out, Chapman. I'm coming for you, and you're going to pay for the crimes laid against you. Lucas Knight.

"Get ready, Chapman," he mumbled as he stared at the message. "Now it's your turn to be hunted, and I'm going to enjoy tracking you down."

Taking a deep breath, Lucas paused only a moment before he hit Send.

SIX

Mia's eyes blinked open, and she sat up in bed with a gasp. For a moment she couldn't remember where she was, and then she rubbed her eyes as the events of the day before trickled back into her memory. She pushed away the thought of the scare she'd had with Tony Chapman and concentrated instead on her arrival at the Knights' home and the welcome she'd received.

With a smile she pulled the covers up around her neck and snuggled down into the warm bed. It had been a long time since she'd awakened and looked forward to the day, but today was different. She was with people she trusted, and Lucas was going to find Tony.

At the thought of Lucas, her heart gave a quick thump, and she wondered when she would see him again. She really needed to go home and get some clothes, but she was afraid to go alone. Tony might be lurking there, waiting for her. But Lucas had other work to do, and she couldn't expect him to drop everything just for her. For now she'd have to make do with the clothes she'd worn when she ran out of her house.

With a sigh she swung her feet over the side of the bed, stood and smoothed out the nightgown Lucas's mother had loaned her. She glanced around the room for her discarded clothes from the night before and was shocked to see them neatly folded and lying on a chair. On top lay a note from Mrs. Knight.

Dear Mia,
I have early duty at the hospital this morning, so I went ahead and laundered your clothes last night. Lucas will be here at nine to pick you up. We will see you tonight. I will be praying that you have a good day.
Rebecca Knight.

Tears flooded Mia's eyes as she finished reading the message. A familiar pain that she'd had since childhood pierced her heart, and she almost doubled over. Was this what having a mother was like? Someone who loved you and took care of your needs even before you realized you had them. Someone who prayed for you to have a good day.

She had very few memories of her mother, who'd died when she was five years old. Would her mother have been like Mrs. Knight? With a sigh she picked up her clothes and headed to the bathroom for a shower, the question unanswered.

Thirty minutes later she walked into the kitchen and stopped in surprise at the sight of Lucas sitting at the kitchen table, his laptop open in front of him. He looked up, and for a moment she thought his eyes lit up when he saw her. Then they shuttered to an impersonal gaze as he nodded at her.

"Good morning. Mom's gone to the hospital, and Dad had to go down to the agency."

She forced herself to smile, suddenly shy at the cool tone of his voice. "Your mom left me a note. What time is it?"

"Almost nine." He pointed toward the coffeepot. "There's coffee, and Mom left some muffins. There's also fruit and yogurt in the refrigerator. What can I get you?"

He started to rise, but she put up her hand to stop him. "No, I'll get it." She walked to the counter where the coffeepot sat and poured some into the cup sitting there. "Can I get you some?"

"I've already had one cup, but I guess a second wouldn't hurt."

He held out his mug, and she refilled it. He'd already directed his attention back to the computer screen by the time she held it out to him. As he reached out to take it, their fingers touched, and a spark like electricity raced from her fingertips up her arm. He jerked his head around to stare at her, and for a moment she stood still, her gaze frozen as his eyes traveled over her face.

He swallowed and eased the cup from her hand before he turned back to stare at the computer. Mia whirled to face the counter, her hands clutching its edges. She closed her eyes and took several deep breaths to still her pounding heart. When her pulse slowed, she picked up her cup, grabbed a muffin and sat down at the table.

Neither one of them spoke for a few minutes. Then Lucas closed the computer before turning to look at her. "How do you feel this morning?"

She swallowed the bite she'd been chewing and nodded. "Fine. I slept really well. When I woke, I found my clothes that your mother had laundered for me. That was so nice of her, but I can't expect her to do that every night. Do you think we could go to my house today and get some of my clothes?"

A slight frown wrinkled his forehead. "I think I'll have time to take you. It all depends..."

The good mood she'd been in ever since awakening drained away at Lucas's hesitant words and distant attitude. What had she expected? Yesterday his kind and chivalrous nature had led her to believe he really cared about what happened to her. Now in the cold light of day she realized she was just another paying client, and she had no right to assume he would be at her beck and call.

Before he could finish what he was saying, she shoved her chair back and pushed to her feet. "No, wait. I said that all wrong. I don't expect you to devote all your time to my case. I can get my clothes by myself. If you'll just drop me off at your house so I can get my car, I'll go. In fact, it might be best if I went home and stayed there."

Lucas's eyebrows shot up. "Stay at home? You can't do that. What if Chapman comes back?"

She shrugged. "I'll keep my doors locked and the security system on. If I hear anything outside, I'll call 911. I'm sure I'll be fine."

Picking up her cup, she strode back to the counter to pour herself a coffee refill. Lucas was out of his chair and standing behind her before she had time to set the cup down. He touched her arm, and she turned to stare at him. "I thought we had this settled yesterday," he said. "If you expect to be safe, you can't stay by yourself until Chapman is back behind bars."

Hoping to see some hint that he was concerned about her welfare, she studied his eyes, but his stony gaze was unreadable. "Why do you care where I stay?"

"Because I don't want you to get hurt."

Tears threatened to flood her eyes, but she blinked them away. "It's not your responsibility to keep me safe, Lucas. You are being paid to find Tony Chapman. I don't expect anything else from you. In fact, I feel really bad about taking advantage of your family last night."

"You didn't take advantage of anything. My parents were glad to have you."

"How could they be, after the way I treated you? They probably don't understand why you took my case. In fact, I'm having trouble understanding it myself. The last time I saw you before yesterday, you told me that you never wanted to see me again. And what did I do? Made a mess out of my life and came running back to your doorstep, begging you to make it right. I can't blame you or your family for not wanting me here."

The muscle in his jaw flexed, and he gritted his teeth. After a moment he exhaled a deep breath and raked his hand through his hair before he spoke. "Mia, sit down. I think we need to talk."

The expression on his face frightened her. She'd been right. He was sorry he was helping her. What was he going to tell her now? That it would be better for her to go to some other agency and get out of his life once more? With shaking fingers, she picked up her cup of coffee and inhaled sharply.

Then she dropped her gaze to the floor and slid into the chair. When he was settled across from her, she glanced back up at him. "All right, Lucas. What is it?"

He bit down on his lip for a moment before he spoke. "I'll admit I've never been as surprised in my life as I was when I opened my door yesterday morning and saw you standing there. At first I was determined that there was no way I could work for you. Then that text came, and I realized you are in real trouble. And I changed my mind. Before the day was over, I knew that I would do whatever it takes to get Chapman off the street. He's already hurt too many people, and I don't want you to be another one on his list."

"Thank you, Lucas, but I'm beginning to think coming to you wasn't the best idea. I was in a state of panic when I left my home, and you were the only one I could think to go to. I never considered your feelings at all. I'm sorry about that. Maybe it would be better for you if I go to another agency."

He shook his head. "No, that's not necessary. I just think we need to set some ground rules here. After all that happened yesterday, we'd gotten comfortable being around each other by last night. Now in the cold light of a new day we're finding it awkward to even look at each other."

"I know. That's why—"

He held up a hand to stop her. "Wait before you say anything else." She pressed her lips together, and he continued. "If anyone had told me a few days ago that I would be sitting in my parents' kitchen having coffee with the woman I once hoped to marry, I would have said they were crazy. But things have changed. I've seen what a monster Chapman can be, and I don't want him to hurt anyone else. So I'm not getting off this case."

She clasped her hands in front of her on the table and leaned forward. "But, Lucas, how do you feel about being around me?"

He exhaled and shook his head. "I don't mind telling you it's hard. I've moved on with my life, and I don't like being reminded of the past. And I don't really know if we can ever put everything that happened between us behind us, but I'd like to try. I'm sorry about what you've had to go through, and I would like to be your friend. Do you think that's possible? Can we be friends after our shared history?"

His gaze didn't waver from her eyes as she mulled over his question. Finally she answered him. "I would like that, but I don't know if it's possible. I'm not sure you will ever want to be friends with me. And I don't blame you for that. I hurt you badly, and it wasn't your fault. No matter how much I regret it, I can't go back and undo it. So if you want to stay on my case, I think we need to just concentrate on your finding Tony."

Lucas gave a curt nod and pursed his lips. "I agree." He pulled his gaze away from her and reached for the notepad he'd written on. "And I know just where to start this morning."

"Where?"

He held up the pad in his hand. "I found

out last night that Chapman has a sister who lives in the city. Her name is Nadine McElroy. I found her address on the internet right before you came into the kitchen. I need to go talk to her. Since I can't leave you here alone, how about coming with me?"

"I'd like that. But it's a little after nine in the morning. Won't anyone who lives there be at work?"

He grinned at her. "It's Saturday. Remember? Hopefully Nadine doesn't work on weekends. So finish your coffee and go get your coat."

She pushed back from the table, reached for her cup and stood. "I'm through. I'll be ready to go in a few minutes."

"I'll take care of the breakfast dishes. You go on and get ready so we can head out."

"Thank you, Lucas."

She turned to leave, but his voice stopped her before she got to the door. "One more thing, Mia."

Turning, she saw that he had also risen and was studying her, his hands jammed into his pockets. "I never know when my job will turn dangerous, and I normally wouldn't take a client with me. But today is different. In case you're worried about going with me, I want you to know that I will protect you from Chapman."

His face flushed, and he shrugged. "I guess I just wanted you to know that I'll do whatever it takes to keep you safe."

The look in his eyes and the almost-whispered tone of his voice hammered at her heart, and she felt the first crack in the ice that had encircled it for years. Her throat clogged with unshed tears, and she tried to smile.

"I never doubted that for a moment. You are a good man."

He smiled, and his blue eyes blazed with a light that almost took her breath away. He cocked his head to one side. "Then what do you say? Let's go catch us a bad guy."

Forty-five minutes later Lucas pulled the car to a stop in front of the address that he'd found for Nadine McElroy. He touched the gun holstered at his waist for reassurance before he turned to Mia.

"Are you ready?"

Her wide eyes stared at the gun partially hidden by the jacket he wore. She glanced up at him and swallowed. "Are you worried you're going to need that?"

He chuckled. "No. Just prepared. I feel undressed if I don't have my gun—a habit that goes back to my days as a SEAL—but I'm not worried about this interview. So don't you worry about it either."

Her shoulders relaxed, and a weak smile pulled at her lips. "Okay. Let's go."

They got out of the car and walked up the sidewalk of the well-kept, neat residence. The minute they stepped onto the porch, a dog began to bark somewhere deep in the house. Lucas pushed the doorbell and took a step back while inside the dog's barks grew louder, closer and more menacing.

After a moment he heard a woman's voice on the other side of the door. "Hush, Chester. Get back."

The door cracked open, and a woman peeked out at them through it. "Yeah? Can I help you?" The dog renewed its barking, and she turned to call over her shoulder. "Bob, come put your dog up. I can't hear myself talk with all this barking."

"Here, boy," a man's voice rang out. The dog quit barking, whirled and ran in the direction of the voice.

The woman opened the door a little wider, and Lucas got a look at her for the first time. She appeared to be in her early forties and had the same dark blond hair that he'd seen in Chapman's mug shot that Scottie Murray had sent him last night. The resemblance ended there. Dark circles lined her eyes, and she had the look of a woman who'd worked hard all her life.

She glanced over her shoulder in the direction where the man and dog had disappeared before she turned back to them. "I'm sorry. That's my husband's dog. I can't do a thing with him, but Bob just has to speak and that dog responds instantly."

"It's okay. We understand." Lucas smiled, hoping to set her at ease. "Are you Mrs. Nadine McElroy?"

She narrowed her eyes and frowned as she let her gaze travel up and down each of them before she spoke. "Yes. What can I do for you?"

"My name is Lucas Knight. I'm a bounty hunter with the Knight Fugitive Recovery Agency, and this is Mia Lockhart. I'm sure you're aware that your brother was granted bail after his arraignment, but he didn't show up for a scheduled court appearance. That makes him a fugitive from justice, and Mrs. Lockhart has hired me to bring him in. We'd like to talk to you if we may."

Her face drained of color, and her mouth dropped open as she reached to close the door. "I don't know anything about Tony, and I don't want to get involved. You should get off my property."

Lucas reached out and placed his palm on the door to keep it from closing. "Mrs. McElroy, we need your help."

"I told you no," she said. "Now, please, leave."

"Just listen to what I have to say. Your brother held an elderly woman hostage yesterday for hours and threatened to kill her. Then he shot two other people at a hotel while trying to abduct Mrs. Lockhart. One of them was seriously injured. It's just a matter of time before he kills someone else, and the more violent his behavior gets, the more likely a shoot-out will occur when the police finally find him. Wouldn't you rather see him in jail than dead?"

The woman hesitated for a moment and bit down on her lip. Footsteps sounded behind her, and a man appeared at her side. He placed his hand on her shoulder, and she moved her head to stare at him. "Let them come in, Nadine. You can't go on protecting Tony forever. It's tearing you apart."

Her body trembled, and she placed her hand on top of his and squeezed. Then, opening the door wider, she turned back to Lucas and Mia. "Come on inside."

They walked through the small entry into a larger room furnished with a sofa and comfortable chairs. A Christmas tree stood in the corner, its lights blinking and reflecting off the bright paper of the wrapped presents underneath. Nadine motioned for Lucas and Mia to sit on the sofa.

She and her husband sat in chairs across from them, and Nadine reached for her husband's hand before she spoke. "This is my husband, Bob. We've been married for twenty-two years and have two teenage sons. I've always tried to keep them from being hurt or embarrassed by anything Tony has done, but after his arrest for murder, I can't do that anymore."

Her husband sighed and shook his head before he looked at Lucas. "I've tried to tell her for years that she can't make Tony change, but she wouldn't believe me. It's like she's been on a mission to get him to redirect his life, and every time he promises to do better, he does something even worse than before instead. Then she feels like it's her fault because she can't make him stop."

Before Lucas could say anything, Mia spoke up. "I understand that, Mrs. McElroy. Through the years he has filled you with a false hope that he could change, if *you* would do this or that. I know how guilty that makes you feel, because I had someone like that in my life. Every time he did something bad, he made me more a victim by telling me that I had failed him in some way, and that was why he kept behaving the way he did. It was never about what *he* had to do to change. Always about what *I* had to do. I've only begun to scratch the surface on why I let that happen and why I didn't break away sooner, and it's going to take a long time for me to put it behind me. But, please, don't let your brother keep making you the victim. He's the only one who can control the choices he makes. You can't do that for him."

Lucas sat in stunned silence at the speech that had just tumbled from Mia's mouth. It seemed Mrs. McElroy was having trouble taking in her words, too. Bob McElroy smiled at Mia and nodded. "That's what I've been telling her for a long time. I hope she'll listen to you."

Nadine pulled her hand free from her husband's grasp, sank back in her chair and rubbed her fingers over her eyes. "I know you're both right. It's just hard to think that the little brother I loved and spoiled could do some of the things he's been accused of. But I have a family I love, and they need to be the most important people in my life. Protecting Tony puts them, and everyone else in Tony's path, at risk." After a moment she took a deep breath, sat up straight and looked at Lucas. "Okay. What do you want to know?"

Lucas scooted to the edge of the couch and stared into her eyes. "First of all, have you had any contact with Tony since he made bail?"

She nodded. "He came by here right after being released and asked to borrow some money. At first I told him I couldn't, and he said he would pay me back, that he had some kind of deal he was working on that was going to make him millions. When I asked him what it was, he said it had to do with a friend of his. He was so insistent that he needed money, and I knew my boys were due home from school. So I finally gave him a few hundred dollars just to get him out of here."

"Did he say where he was going to stay until this deal came through?"

"He said he'd be at Clyde's house until he had the money in hand, then he would be leaving. I asked him about the murder charges, and he said he didn't intend to go back to jail."

Lucas pulled the notepad from his pocket. "And who is Clyde?"

"Clyde Harper. He's a former cellmate of Tony's."

"Do you know where he lives?"

She shook her head. "No, but I think he works in a bar on the south side of town. Tony told me the name one time." She frowned and pursed her lips as she concentrated. After a moment she shrugged. "I'm not sure, but I think it's the Lion's Den."

Lucas wrote the name down. "We'll check him out. Can you give me a description of what he looks like?"

Nadine grimaced and frowned. "Last summer, when Tony brought him by here, I'll never forget how scared I was just looking at him." She studied Lucas for a moment. "He was about your height, maybe weighed a bit more, but it was his eyes that caught my attention. They had an evil spark to them that sent chills down my back. He was bald, and the T-shirt he wore showed off a tattoo that set my teeth on edge. It was a coiled snake that curved from the back of his head and ran down his neck, onto his arm and all the way to his wrist. You won't have any trouble recognizing him."

"Sounds like a guy I wouldn't want to meet in a dark alley," Lucas said as he recorded the description. Then he glanced back at Nadine. "Now, about that deal your brother was working on. Did he ever tell you who he was work-ing with? Could it have been Clyde?"

She shook her head and chuckled. "From the way Tony talked, it was something that had taken months to plan and implement. Clyde isn't smart or patient enough for something like that. So if he was involved, it was more a matter of needing an extra hired gun. I got the impres-sion that his partner on the deal was a young yuppie that he'd gotten mixed up with." She glanced at Mia. "I can't prove it, but I think it was your husband, Mrs. Lockhart."

"Why do you think that?" Lucas asked.

"Because I heard him talking on the phone once, and he sounded upset. I heard him say the name Kyle, but I didn't know anybody by that name." She paused. "Not until Tony was arrested."

Lucas nodded and wrote the information on the notepad before he continued. "Speaking of phone calls," he said, "the lady that your brother held hostage yesterday said that he called you while he was there. What did he want?"

Nadine glanced down at her feet and swal-lowed before she answered. "He wanted what he always wants from me—money. He said a deal he'd been working on had been delayed, but he said he expected it to be resolved any minute. He said when it was, he'd be able to pay me back everything I'd ever loaned him."

"What did you tell him?"

She glanced at her husband and then to Lucas. "I told him I didn't have any extra cash right then, but I would by the end of next week if he could wait that long."

"What did he say?" Lucas asked.

"He said that he thought his deal would be finished by then and he wouldn't need the money by that time. I was getting ready for him to begin making me feel guilty about not giving anything to him when all of a sudden he seemed in a hurry to get off the phone. He said he had to go, that he'd talk to me later, and disconnected the call."

"That's probably when he saw my car pulling out of the driveway," Lucas said. "And you haven't heard from him since?"

Nadine shook her head. "No." Tears filled her eyes, and she clasped her hands in her lap as she stared at Mia. "I really am sorry about your husband, Mrs. Lockhart."

Lucas glanced at Mia, but her face betrayed no emotion. He turned his attention back to Nadine. "Do you know the names of any more of your brother's friends?"

"No, but Clyde might, if he'll talk to you. But be careful about approaching him. I think he's a dangerous man."

"We will be," Lucas said as he rose to his feet. "Thank you for giving us Clyde Harper's name. Maybe he can lead us to where your brother is. But I would caution you. Tony is a fugitive from the law, and you need to call the police if he shows up again. If you let him in, you could be charged with harboring a wanted criminal. I'm sure you don't want that to happen to your family."

Nadine shook her head. "No, I don't. I'll remember what you said."

Lucas and Mia walked to the door and stopped as Nadine opened it for them. "Thank you, Nadine, for seeing us today," Mia said.

Nadine smiled at her and squeezed her arm. "Thank you for what you said about not being the victim anymore. I'll remember that."

Mia smiled and nodded before walking out the door. Lucas followed her to the car, and they got inside without speaking. When he cranked the engine, he let it idle for a moment as he stared at his hands on the steering wheel. Then he turned to face Mia. "I was surprised at what you said to Nadine about people making choices. I'm glad you're beginning to see that the things Kyle did were his fault, not yours."

She swiveled in the seat toward him. "I saw the pain in her face. It was very much like what I've felt for years. I know I have a lot of emotional healing to do, and I've been trying to do something about it. I've started going to a group for abused women, and it's helping me deal with my issues. But I still have a ways to go."

Her words surprised him, and his mouth gaped open. "How long have you been going?"

"I began right after Kyle's death. I saw an ad on TV about a group that met in a church near my house, and I went. It's been good for me."

"That's great, Mia. I'm so proud of you."

Her cheeks flushed, and she dipped her head to stare at her hands. "It's just something I felt like I had to do."

Lucas reached over and covered her hands with his. "There are a lot of women who wouldn't have done that. I was right last night when I said you are strong."

She glanced up then, her eyes seeming to beg for him to reassure her. "Do you mean that?"

He chucked her under the chin and smiled. "I do. You remind me of that girl who was once a Sugar Plum Fairy."

"I was afraid that girl was gone forever," she said. "I hope I can bring her back."

His fingers still touched her chin, and he knew he should pull them away, but he couldn't. "Don't worry," he whispered. "We'll find her." She just nodded, and after a moment he sat up straight. "Now why don't we go get your clothes?"

She breathed a sigh of relief. "Yes, let's do that. And I can get..." She bit down on her lip as if to cut off her words.

"Get what?" he asked.

"Something that I didn't take with me when I ran out of the house."

He arched an eyebrow. "It sounds like it's important."

"It is to me. It wouldn't be to anybody else."

"Okay," he said, "now you have me hooked. You have to tell me what it is."

She rolled her eyes and then glared at him. "Nothing you would be interested in. Now can we just go?"

Lucas grinned and shook his head. "Oh, no. You're not going to put me off like that. What is it?"

Her face grew redder. "Lucas, quit teasing me and just drive."

Now he couldn't resist finding out what she

was hiding from him. "We're not going a foot until you tell me what you just have to get at your house."

She clenched her fists. "All right. If you must know, it's the stuffed bear my mother gave me for Christmas when I was four. She died a few months later, and it's the only thing I have to remember her by."

"A stuffed bear?"

"Yes," she hissed. "It's my most treasured possession."

His eyes widened in surprise. "Did you have it when we were in college?"

"Of course I did. But what girl wants to tell her boyfriend she still has a stuffed bear that sits on the table beside her bed every night?"

"So it's more than just a childhood toy. It's a reminder of the last Christmas you spent with your mother."

She gave a nervous laugh and glanced at him. "It's the only Christmas I remember. I never had one after that. My father thought it was a waste of time."

His eyes grew wide. "You never celebrated Christmas or received presents when you were a child?"

She shook her head. "Oh, I got presents. My father saw that my nanny bought me lots of toys. I'd open them with her on Christmas morning before she left to spend the day with her family. But my father was never there, and I spent the day alone in a big house with servants who were paid to watch me. When I saw that Christmas tree at your parents' home last night and listened to all of you talk about the dinner your mother is planning for the family on Christmas Day, I wondered if you and your brother and sister really know how incredibly lucky you are. I never had anything like that."

His stomach roiled, and he swallowed. He'd thought he had known all about Mia's life at one time, but now he realized there was much she had never shared with him. She hadn't had a mother's love, or a father who gave her any attention, or a husband who loved her. But the question that pulled at his heart was, had he been any better than others in her life who'd let her down? At the time he'd been so obsessed with becoming a navy SEAL that he hadn't given a thought to how Mia felt about his plans. Had he been so focused on his own dreams and goals that he hadn't considered hers at all? He didn't know, but it was something he was sure he would think about in days to come.

She had her head bowed, and her hair hung down the side of her face. He reached over and tucked a strand behind her ear. She glanced around at him, and he smiled. "I'm sorry I teased you. Don't worry. We'll get your bear."

She breathed a sigh of relief as he drove away from the McElroys' home. They rode in a comfortable silence for a few miles before she spoke. "Lucas, it's been so good to be with you these last two days. Thank you for helping me."

"It's been good for me, too, Mia. I think we're on the way to being friends after all."

"I think so, too."

Twenty minutes later they pulled up in front of Mia's house and climbed from the car. Mia grabbed her keys from her pocket and headed to the door. Lucas had just stepped up on the front porch behind her when he heard her gasp.

He looked over her shoulder and froze at the sight of the front door hanging on its hinges. He pushed Mia behind him and pulled out his gun. Holding it with both hands, he stepped inside the entry to sweep the room and stopped in shock at the sight before him.

SEVEN

Mia heard Lucas gasp, and she stepped closer to him as she clutched at the back of his jacket. He didn't move for a moment, and then he dug in his jeans pocket and pulled something out. Reaching behind him, he shoved his car keys in her hand.

"Take these," he whispered. "I'm going inside. Get in my car, lock the doors and call the police. Start the engine, and at the first hint of trouble, get out of here."

She looked down at the keys she was now holding, and her fingers tightened around them. "What's wrong?" she whispered.

"Your house looks like it's been ransacked. I don't know if whoever did this is still here, but I need to check. Now go on back to the car."

Her knees began to shake. She didn't know if her legs would support her to get back to the car. And even if she made it to safety, what about Lucas? A burglar intent on breaking into her home probably wouldn't hesitate to attack anyone attempting to stop him. The thought of Lucas being hurt sent cold chills down her spine.

"Lucas, be careful."

He gave a quick glance over his shoulder and nodded. "I will. Now, please, go back to the car."

Mia backed away and ran down the steps. She had the key in the ignition, and the engine started almost before she had the car door closed. Her right hand shook as she rested it on the gear shift, the other one clutching the steering wheel. Her heart hammered in her ears as she watched Lucas disappear into the house.

The minutes seemed to drag as she stared at the front door, hoping to see Lucas emerge, but he didn't reappear. How long had he been inside? Had the intruder attacked him? Was he lying hurt somewhere? Should she go in search of him?

She couldn't pull her gaze away from the front door as these questions raced through her mind. So focused on keeping watch was she that the sudden tapping on the window of the driver's side door sent a shock wave of panic spiraling through her. Her scream split the air as she whirled to face the person standing outside the car.

Relief flowed through her at the sight of Lucas's surprised face staring at her through the glass. Before she knew what she was doing, she opened the door, jumped outside and threw her arms around his neck.

"Oh, Lucas," she sobbed. "I was so worried about you."

His body stiffened for a moment, and then he relaxed as his arms came up to embrace her. "I'm sorry, Mia. I didn't mean to scare you. I came out the back door of the house and around to the front. I thought you saw me come around the corner."

She couldn't seem to let go of him and hugged him tighter. "No, I didn't see you. I had convinced myself that you were lying inside hurt."

He chuckled and shook his head. "No, I'm fine. Whoever did the damage inside is long gone."

Suddenly Mia realized that she and Lucas were standing in an embrace, and her face grew warm. Releasing her hold on him, she stepped back out of his arms and tried to smile. "I'm sorry to act like such a scared child." She glanced toward the house. "So you say the place is in shambles?"

He swallowed, the muscles in his throat constricting, and took a deep breath. "Yeah, I'm afraid so. Let's go in and see how much damage was done. We'll clean it up after the police have had a chance to look it over."

Together they walked up the steps and entered the house. Mia stopped inside the door and let her gaze drift over the interior. The cushions of the sofa and chairs in the living room had been cut open, and the foam and batting from inside lay scattered across the floor. Pictures had been ripped from the walls that were now dotted with gaping holes.

As she walked through the house, she discovered that no room had escaped the same destruction. Everywhere she looked, everything lay broken and shattered.

Lucas stood silently behind her as she surveyed the damage. "I'm so sorry, Mia," he said.

She didn't respond for a moment as she let her gaze drift over the wreckage of what had once been a state-of-the art kitchen. "It doesn't matter. I hated this house and the life I lived here. It's as if the house finally became as broken as I was when I lived in it." She turned around and faced Lucas. "Do you think Tony did this?"

"He's at the top of my suspect list."

She frowned. "I know he's angry at me for burning him. But why would he go to such extremes to destroy my house?"

"Because he's looking for something. The thing that he keeps asking you about."

Mia held up her hands in despair. "But I don't have any idea what he's talking about. Why won't he believe me?"

"Because whatever it is must be very valuable. Like Nadine said, Chapman thought it was going to earn him millions, and she suspected that Kyle was in on it with him. Maybe Kyle was killed because he had double-crossed Chapman, and now Chapman wants all the money to himself." He frowned and tilted his head to one side as he studied her face. "Are you sure Kyle never mentioned anything to you?"

She snorted in disgust. "Kyle never talked to me about anything. But I wouldn't put it past him to be involved in something illegal and with someone like Tony Chapman."

Lucas nodded. "That seems to make sense." Then he inhaled a deep breath. "What do you want to do about the house? I'll help you clean it up if that's what you want. Or I know some guys who own a company that cleans out old houses before renovation work starts. I could probably get them to come sort everything out that needs to be thrown away."

Mia rubbed her hands across her eyes and sighed. "That sounds like a good idea. This place won't be livable again until it's cleaned up. On the other hand, I don't know if I ever want to come back here to live."

"If you don't come back, where will you go?"

She shrugged. "I don't know. But I do know that there are too many horrible memories associated with this place. I had intended to sell it when the estate was settled anyway. I suppose there are a lot of decisions I'll have to make in the future, but I don't want to think about that until Tony is caught."

"Well, you don't have to worry about the house right now," Lucas said. "You have a place to stay for the time being, and we'll figure something out when Chapman's back behind bars."

Her heart twisted at how he'd said *we* will figure things out. It might have been a slip of the tongue, but to Mia it reminded her that for the time being she wasn't alone. Of course it would be different after Lucas finished this job for her, but she wouldn't think about that now. Plenty of time to do that later on.

Taking a deep breath, she turned and smiled at him. "Let's go see how badly damaged my bedroom is."

She headed down a hallway that led to the master bedroom, with Lucas following behind her. Like the rest of the house, it had been trashed. The drawers to the dresser had been pulled out and their contents scattered across the floor. The mattress had been moved from the bed and cut open. Clothes from the closet littered the floor.

In the middle of all the chaos Mia spotted the bear her mother had given her lying on his side, partially covered by a dress that had been thrown from the closet. A gasp escaped her throat, and she stooped down to pick up the stuffed animal, half expecting to see his body sliced open. To her amazement the bear appeared to be unharmed, and she hugged him close to her chest before she held him out for Lucas to see.

"This is Teddy," she said.

His mouth twisted in a teasing smile. "Unusual name for a teddy bear."

She arched her eyebrows and stared down her nose. "I was four years old when I named him."

He studied the bear a moment more. "He has an eye missing."

"I know. I did eye surgery on him when I was five, but I could never reattach the eye."

A smile pulled at Lucas's lips. "Poor Teddy. I'm sure he's forgiven you."

Tears filled her eyes as she turned to Lucas. "I hope so. He's my dearest possession. I don't know how he escaped being mutilated, but I'm so glad he did. This is the only thing in this house that I care about."

Lucas stared at her, his blue eyes filled with an intense look that made her breathless with a longing that she hadn't experienced in years. For an instant she was again that young college girl, a ballerina who dreamed of owning a dance studio and sharing her life with the free-spirited young man ready to serve his country in the navy SEALs. Then reality crashed in on her, and her stomach roiled. They would never be those two idealistic young people again. Too much had happened. And it was all her fault.

Tears filled her eyes, and she turned away to keep Lucas from seeing them. The overturned bedside table lay on its side next to the closet, and she walked over and set it upright. Then she placed the bear on it and took a deep breath before she faced Lucas.

"I suppose I should pick out a few clothes to pack, but I need to get my suitcase."

Lucas glanced from her to the bear before he cleared his throat. "Where is it? I'll get it for you."

"It's in the attic. There's a pull-down ladder in the garage to get up there. Come on, and I'll show you the way."

They hadn't been into the garage since coming into the house, but Mia wasn't surprised to see that it hadn't escaped her intruder either. Several boxes of Kyle's things that she'd put there until she could take them to Goodwill had been emptied, their contents strewn across the concrete floor. Tools and cleaning supplies that had once sat on shelves had also been dumped across the area. The ladder leading to the attic had been pulled down to provide access to the storage area above, and through the yawning hole in the ceiling Mia saw that the attic light had been left on.

Lucas motioned her to stand aside as he put his foot on the bottom rung. "I'll check out the attic. You wait here."

She held her breath as he climbed up the ladder. His footsteps echoed overhead as he moved about. After a few moments she called out to him. "Lucas, are you okay?"

"Yeah," he answered. "Your visitor went through everything up here, too. I'm looking for your suitcase. What color is it?"

"Black leather, medium-sized. If you don't find it, it's no big deal. I can grab a garbage bag or something to stuff some clothes in."

"Don't do that. I'll keep looking."

"Okay," she answered. "But I'm going back in the bedroom to start figuring out what I want to take."

"I'll be there in a few minutes."

Turning, she walked through the door that led from the garage into the utility room and stopped when she entered the kitchen. Her eye caught sight of a photograph lying amid the broken dishes from the cabinet, and she bent to pick it up. She blinked in surprise at a picture of her and Lucas from when they were in college. He had his arm around her shoulders, and they smiled at the camera, their happiness at being together evident on their faces.

She had no idea where the picture had been all these years or how it ended up amidst the rubble in her kitchen. Standing back up, she stared at the picture as she brushed her fingertips across it. They had been on a picnic with friends at Overton Park when that picture was taken, just weeks before she and Lucas had quarreled about whether they should get married before or after he enlisted in the navy through the SEAL Challenge Contract. He'd wanted to wait, and she'd been against it. He'd left for boot camp, and she'd met Kyle. End of story, and beginning of a lifetime of regret for her.

She shook her head and shoved the picture in her jeans pocket. Sighing, she turned to go toward the bedroom and froze in terror.

A man stood a few feet away.

She'd never seen him before, but she knew immediately who he was. He wore a heavy coat, but no hat covered his bald head with the elaborate snake tattoo that Nadine McElroy had described. Her breath hitched in her throat at the sight of the gun he held.

"So you're Lockhart's wife?" he rasped.

Mia took a step back and came to a stop when the counter pressed against her. "And you're Clyde Harper. Wh-what do you want with me?"

"It's not me, honey. It's my friend Tony. He's very anxious for you to see the marks you left on him."

Her eyes grew wide as a scream ripped from her throat. Before she could move, Clyde had grabbed her around the waist, trapping her arms against her sides, and hoisted her in his arms. She kicked and tried to wedge herself loose, but it was no use.

Another scream tore from her throat, and he drew an arm back and slammed the gun against the side of her head. Pain exploded behind her eyes, and her head lolled against his shoulders. She struggled to scream again, but no sound emerged from her throat.

With a sinking heart, she realized she was being half carried and half dragged out the doors that led to the patio and across the back-yard toward the lake. Through her glazed vision she spotted the outline of a boat at the private dock behind the house. She had to do something before he dumped her in the boat and made his escape, but her head hurt, mud-dling her thoughts. They were only a few feet away from the dock when she felt herself being shifted over the man's shoulders. Her head and arms dangled over his back as she stared down-ward at the ground. Three gunshots split the air, and then there was only darkness.

Lucas spotted the edge of what looked like a leather suitcase hidden underneath a pile of blankets and pulled the bag loose. He was headed back to the ladder when he heard a sound that caused him to stop and tilt his head to one side. Was that a scream?

He threw the suitcase aside and lunged toward the ladder. He was halfway down when he heard another scream. There was no mistaking it. That had been Mia's voice. His senses surged to high alert as he jumped off the ladder to the floor and pulled his gun from its holster.

He burst through the door from the garage into the kitchen and yelled. "Mia! Where are you?"

Only silence greeted him. Pressing his lips together in a grim line, he gripped his gun tighter and eased toward the doorway that led into the den. A gust of wind blew across the room at that moment, and he whirled to face the glass doors that led to the patio. He was certain they'd been closed before, but now one stood open.

He charged across the room and burst through the doorway onto the patio. His eyes widened in disbelief as he spotted a heavyset, muscular man holding what appeared to be an unconscious Mia in his arms and running toward a small motorboat at the dock. Reaching in his pocket, he pulled out his cell phone and punched the app that sent an SOS of his location to his office, the signal that he needed police backup immediately.

Then he sprinted forward. "Stop!" he yelled at the top of his voice.

The man glanced around, hoisted Mia over his shoulder and turned to point a gun in his direction. His naval training kicked in, and Lucas instinctively threw himself to the ground as a bullet whizzed over his head.

Lucas raised his gun to fire but hesitated. With Mia draped over the man's shoulder, he risked hitting her if he aimed for her captor. He had only a split second to decide what to do before he racked the gun's slide and fired at the boat. The bullet pierced the hull near the waterline, and even at the distance he was from the dock Lucas could see the gaping, jagged hole it left. Another shot nearer the waterline produced an even larger hole. The faint smell of gasoline drifted on the breeze, and Lucas knew he'd hit the gas tank.

The man whirled, and for the first time Lucas caught sight of his tattoo. Clyde Harper. So Chapman had sent his hired hand to do his dirty work.

Holding the gun steady, Lucas pushed to his feet and inched forward. "You're not going to make it across the lake in that boat, Harper. So put the gun down and let the girl go."

Clyde's face filled with rage as he spun back to face Lucas. His hand twitched, and he appeared to be undecided. He glanced at the boat and then toward the tree line to the right of Mia's property. He raised the gun once more but didn't fire.

Lucas took a step closer. "You don't need to die here today, but that's what's going to happen if you don't do as I say."

Clyde cast one more glance at his disabled boat and let out an angry roar as he shoved his gun into Mia's ribs. "No! You don't want her to die, so you're going to do what *I* say. Now, get out of my way." Still holding the gun on Mia, he began to back toward the tree line. "You won't shoot and risk hitting her, so I guess I'll have to leave by an alternate route."

Lucas grasped his gun with both hands and stared down the barrel. "Don't be an idiot. You can't get far in those woods carrying the dead-weight of an unconscious hostage. The police will have you in custody before you get to the main road."

Clyde chuckled. "I'll be long gone before they get here."

Lucas shook his head. "No, you won't.

They've already been alerted, and they should be on their way here now. If you surrender now and tell the police what you know about Kyle Lockhart's murder, I'll help you."

Clyde's mouth tightened into a grim line. "I don't know nothing about a murder," he snarled.

"Then why are you so intent on kidnapping the murdered man's widow? Think, Clyde. You try to escape, and you're going to be charged as an accessory to murder and anything else Tony Chapman has done since jumping bail. Do you want to go back to prison?"

His hand holding the gun wobbled, and he swallowed. "No."

"Then cooperate with us, and I'll talk with the DA about giving you immunity."

"I don't need your help," Clyde growled.

"Yes, you do. You may have started out to help your friend with a deal he had going with Kyle Lockhart, but now there's Kyle's murder to account for. And kidnapping Kyle's wife and shooting me will only make matters worse. You'll be lucky if you ever see the outside of a prison again. But it doesn't have to come to that."

Clyde swallowed. "What do you mean?"

"Tell the police where they can find Tony and what he and Lockhart were involved in.

You can have a get-out-of-jail-free card if you just cooperate."

"I don't know…" He stopped and turned his head slightly as the sound of sirens drifted on the air.

Lucas raised his gun and stared down the barrel. "That's the police, Clyde. Make up your mind now. You can lay the girl and the gun down now and take the easy way out, or you can choose the hard way. Which is it going to be?"

Indecision lined Clyde's face as the shrill sound of sirens drew nearer. He glanced over his shoulder as if gauging his chances of escaping through the forest. Then he exhaled a deep breath and released his hold on Mia. She slid down his body and landed in a heap on the ground.

Clyde dropped his gun and raised his hands. "I can't go back to jail. I wouldn't make it in there again. I'll tell the police whatever they want to know about Lockhart and Tony."

Lucas stepped forward and kicked Clyde's gun out of his reach. "You've made the right choice, Clyde. Now get down on your knees and put your hands behind your head. The police should be here any minute."

Clyde nodded, raised his arms and locked his

hands behind his head. "None of this was my idea. I should never have let Tony talk me into it. I knew Lockhart and that other guy were bad news the first time I saw them."

"What other guy?" Lucas asked.

"The one who is the brains in the whole smuggling operation."

Lucas's eyebrows shot up. "Smuggling? Lockhart was involved in smuggling? Who was the man in charge?"

Clyde opened his mouth, but before he could speak, two gunshots rang out from the forest. A stunned expression flashed across Clyde's face as he clutched at his chest, and then fell facedown onto the ground.

A third shot kicked up dirt at Lucas's feet, and he nose-dived to the ground, covering Mia's body with his. He cringed as a fourth shot hit the earth just inches from where they lay. He cradled Mia closer as the fifth shot went wide. He braced himself, wondering where the next bullet would land, but there was silence from the forest.

In the distance, he heard car doors slam and voices calling out. He raised his head a few inches and spied four police officers, one with a K-9 dog on a leash, rounding the corner of the house.

Lucas laid his gun on the ground and raised his hands in the air as he pushed to his knees. "I'm Lucas Knight, a bounty hunter, in the pursuit of a bail jumper. There's a shooter in the forest!" he yelled to the approaching officers.

"I know Lucas!" one of the officers yelled, confirming his story as they ran forward.

Three of the policemen ran past and into the woods, but the one who'd recognized Lucas stopped, knelt next to Clyde and searched for a pulse in his neck. After a moment he shook his head and spoke into his lapel mic as he called for an ambulance. Then he looked up. "He's gone. What happened here, Lucas?"

Lucas pushed into a sitting position and pulled Mia into his arms. "This guy ransacked the house and tried to kidnap Mrs. Lockhart."

The officer listened as Lucas explained the events that had occurred at the house, beginning with their arrival and concluding with Clyde's attempt to escape through the forest. "I thought I had him talked into giving himself up when someone in the woods shot him in the back. It must have been his partner, who didn't want to take a chance on him talking to the police."

The officer leaned closer and stared down at Mia. "Is she wounded?"

Lucas shook his head. "I don't know. She's been unconscious for the last ten minutes—and I don't know how she got that way. I don't think a bullet struck her, but she may have hit her head."

The officer pushed to his feet. "Dispatch had gotten the call that a burglary had been reported, and officers were on their way when the second call came in. An ambulance should be here any moment. I'm going to find the guys in the woods and relay the information you've given me and then see if I'm needed to look for the shooter. Will you be okay staying with her until the EMTs get here?"

Lucas bit down on his lip and nodded as he tightened his hold on Mia. The sensation of helplessness he'd felt when he'd walked out of the house and seen Clyde carrying Mia washed back over him. Now as he held her in his arms and stared down into her face, the need to protect her warred with his earlier determination to treat Mia no differently than he did any other client.

But he could no longer fool himself into thinking that she meant no more to him than a stranger, and he knew it. Just as surely as he'd known for years that he'd been kidding himself that he'd overcome his feelings for her.

In the deep recesses of his soul, he'd always known the truth. Mia owned his heart and always would.

All the anger he'd felt for her over the past seven years melted away as he stared down into her still face. Then, pulling her closer, he pressed his lips to her forehead. "Mia, please, wake up."

She stirred in his arms, and her forehead wrinkled. He leaned back and looked down into her eyes. Mia was staring up at him, a frown on her face. "L-Lucas, wh-where am I?"

He released a breath in relief and tried to smile. "We're in your backyard. Clyde Harper tried to abduct you, but you're okay now."

She raised a hand and rubbed her eyes. "I don't remember."

Before Lucas could respond, two EMTs ran around the corner of the house. "Don't worry about it now. We'll talk about it later."

He released her and stood as the EMTs came to a stop beside them. Then, backing away, he watched while one checked Clyde's body, the other examining Mia. A noise behind him alerted him to the return of the officers from the woods, and he swiveled to meet them.

"Did you find the shooter?"

The officer in charge shook his head. "No."

He pointed to the dog, whose handler was patting him. "Rocket trailed him through the forest and about a half mile over to the next house on the lake, where he lost the trail. The guy must have had a car there."

Lucas nodded. "I suspected as much. But if his partner was only half a mile away, why did he come in a boat and where did he get it?"

"We know where he got it. The next house over has a boat dock, and we talked to the owner. She said she'd just discovered the boat had been stolen and was about to make a police report when we arrived." The officer shrugged. "As to why he used a boat, I don't know. Maybe he didn't want to carry Mrs. Lockhart that distance, or maybe he thought the authorities wouldn't think to look for him out on the water. I guess if we find the shooter, we'll know."

Lucas was about to ask another question when one of the EMTs spoke up behind him. "We've got Mrs. Lockhart ready to go to the hospital, and we need to leave with her. The other victim was already dead when we arrived. So we'll leave him for the crime scene investigators."

The officer nodded. "Thanks, guys."

"Do you need me for anything else, or can I go with Mia to the hospital?" Lucas asked.

The officer shook his head. "I think you've told us enough for now, but the detectives may want to talk to you later."

Lucas pulled his card from his pocket and handed it to the man. "They can reach me there. I know most of the detectives on the force. In fact, my brother-in-law is Ryan Spencer."

The officer looked at the card, and his eyebrows arched. "Oh, you're one of the Knights? I've heard about your agency. Go on with Mrs. Lockhart, and we'll check with you later."

Lucas glanced over his shoulder and saw that the EMTs were already pushing the gurney with Mia on it toward the house. He started after them but had taken only a few steps when he stopped and turned back to the officer who was crouched down beside Clyde's body.

"Just out of curiosity, could you tell me who is the owner of the house where the boat was stolen?"

The man looked up and nodded. "Sure. It's Christine Abbott."

A cold chill ran down Lucas's spine at the name. "Christine Abbott, the hotel heiress?" The woman beside Kyle in all those newspaper photos from a string of public events?

The officer's blank face stared back at him.

"I don't know about that. I just know that's her name."

Lucas nodded and walked slowly toward the house, the pictures in the report Scottie Murray had sent him flashing through his mind. There had been something about the shots of Christine Abbott and Kyle Lockhart that hinted at more than a business relationship. Maybe it had been the looks they directed at each other or the way her hand seemed so at ease on Kyle's arm, almost like a caress. Or the way their shoulders touched in almost every picture.

If there had been a more intimate relationship between the two, then maybe they had also been partners in whatever Kyle had been involved in. And the fact that the boat to be used to help abduct Mia came from her dock seemed too much of a coincidence.

Clyde had said something about smuggling before he died, and what better place to do it than an import business? And what better partner than a wealthy socialite who could provide money needed to help assure safe passage through the black market channels into the country?

Smuggling, a killer wanting something Kyle had hidden, and a wealthy socialite. With those three clues, Lucas at last had a lead to follow to find Chapman and help Mia. At the thought of Mia, he jogged forward and rounded the house just as the ambulance pulled away.

He headed to his car but stopped before getting in. His knees suddenly wobbled, and he reached out to catch hold of the car door. Mia could have been killed a few minutes ago, and it had opened his eyes to what he'd long tried to deny. He had never quit loving her.

On the other hand, she had hurt him deeply when she'd turned her back on him for Kyle Lockhart. He'd brooded about that for years, and he didn't know if he could ever fully trust her again. What would happen when she no longer needed him? That was a question he couldn't answer.

They both had a lot of healing to do. Maybe neither one of them would ever be able to overcome what they'd suffered since their college days. Only time would tell. Right now she needed a friend, and that's what he would be.

He opened the car door and started to get in but stopped and glanced at the house. As a friend, there was one thing he could do for her. He closed the door and headed back into the house to find the one thing that brought her comfort, her teddy bear.

EIGHT

Mia sat up on the side of the bed in the emergency room cubicle where she'd been since arriving at the hospital and touched the bandage that covered the side of her head. The pain medication the nurse had given her had kicked in, and the room seemed to tilt.

She hated being in a hospital. It reminded her of all the visits she'd made in the past and her feeble attempts to explain away her bruises and injuries. Now as she thought about it, she wondered how she had ever convinced herself that she'd fooled the hospital staff into believing the stories Kyle had made her tell. After all, there had to be a limit to how many times even the clumsiest individual could fall down a flight of steps or walk into the corner of an open door.

To the credit of the doctors and nurses she'd seen on those visits, she had always been counseled about what she needed to do to protect herself from further abuse, but it had done no good. She had wanted so badly for her life to be different, and she had convinced herself to believe Kyle's promises that he would never assault her again. But there had always been a next time, and each one worse than the one before.

Tears filled her eyes. With an angry swipe she brushed her cheeks and took a deep breath. Kyle was never going to hurt her again, but it wasn't so easy to forget what had happened in the past. Time was what she needed. Quiet, peaceful, stress-free time—which she would never get until Tony Chapman was back in jail. Once she was safe, she'd be able to get on with her life. But what kind of life would she have? What did she have to fill it? A home that she hated. No job. No family. No friends.

Movement at the door caught her attention, and she darted a glance in that direction. Her pulse beat out a staccato rhythm when Lucas walked into the room. His forehead wrinkled, and his gaze raked her as if he was trying to convince himself she was all right.

He walked across the room and stopped in front of her. Her breath hitched in her throat as he reached up and touched her cheek just below where the bandage on the side of her head ended. His fingers trailed down to her face, and he cupped his hand around the curve of her jaw.

"I'm so sorry he hurt you," he rasped. "It's all my fault. I shouldn't have left you alone."

Mia reached up and covered his hand with hers. "It's not your fault. We had no idea Clyde was anywhere around. I should have waited until you came back down from the attic. But if I had, he might have shot you and then kidnapped me. Tell me what happened. I remember him taking me out the patio door and hitting me on the head. The next thing I remember is waking up with your..." She hesitated. She had intended to say "with your lips on my forehead," but she didn't. "With you holding me."

Lucas nodded. "Well, it's kind of a long story. How about my telling you about it on our way to my parents' home? You're being released, and my mom is expecting us. I told the doctor you'd have your own private nurse until you're feeling better."

"I feel fine now, and I'm ready to get out of this place. I don't like hospitals. They remind me of... Well, never mind what they remind me of. I just don't like hospitals."

He smiled, and his eyes narrowed a bit. "I understand."

"Can I leave now?"

"You can." When she started to climb down from the table, he reached out and placed his hands on her waist. She'd forgotten how strong he was until he lifted her as if she was light as a feather and set her feet on the ground. He held on to her for a few seconds as if to see if she could stand alone before he released her. "My car is outside."

He took her hand and led her from the room to the nurses' station. A nurse came around the desk when she spotted them. "Mrs. Lockhart, all your paperwork is complete, and I have a wheelchair ready to take you to the exit." She glanced at Lucas. "You can go get your car and pull around to the double doors. We'll wait for you there."

"Okay." He held Mia's arm as she sat down in the wheelchair. Then he bent over and gave her hand a squeeze. "I'll be waiting for you in the car."

She smiled up at him. "Thank you, Lucas. You've been wonderful today."

"Don't mention it. You're easy to be nice to."

She watched as he turned and hurried down the hallway. When he'd exited the ER, the nurse grabbed the handles of the wheelchair. "Are you ready to go?"

"I am."

"The doctor gave you a prescription for some pain medication, if you need it tonight. Your friend said he'd get it filled on the way home," the nurse said as she pushed her down the hallway.

"Thank you, but I feel fine now."

"I'm glad, but you never can tell how you'll feel later. You have a nasty bump on your head. Your young man was quite concerned when he arrived. He paced back and forth in the waiting room the entire time he was here until he was allowed back to see you."

Mia's face warmed, and she tried to suppress the smile that wanted to spread across her face. "He's not my young man. He's a good friend who's helping with a problem in my life. In fact, he saved my life today. I'm very grateful."

They had reached the exit by this time, and Mia caught sight of Lucas pulling to a stop outside. The nurse chuckled as Lucas jumped from the car and hurried back toward the exit. "Not your young man, huh? I see friends of patients all the time in my job, and I'd say that man coming toward you right now has more than friendship on his mind." She leaned forward and whispered in Mia's ear. "Take my word for it."

Mia started to respond, but Lucas opened the door for the nurse to push her outside. When they stopped at the car, Lucas put his arm around Mia's waist and helped her to her feet. Then, supporting her weight against his side, he opened the car door and held on to her until she was safely seated. Once she was settled, he turned and smiled to the nurse.

"Thank you for all your help."

"You're welcome," she answered. "And you have the prescription?"

He nodded. "I do. I'll get it filled on the way home."

Lucas still held the car door open, and the nurse leaned over to speak to Mia. "Good luck. I'm glad you're getting to go home. Just take it easy for a few days." She glanced over her shoulder at Lucas. "And don't forget what I told you."

Mia smiled and nodded as the woman stepped back and Lucas closed the door. Then Lucas was in the car, and they were pulling out into the late afternoon traffic. "What a day," he said.

Lucas directed his attention to the street in front of them and didn't say anything else as they drove toward his parents' home. Mia leaned back in the seat and closed her eyes, her mind returning to the way Lucas had stared down at her after he'd pulled his lips away from her forehead.

Her heart hammered at the memory, and she clasped her curled fists in her lap. Thoughts like that would only end up getting her hurt. Lucas had made it clear he only wanted to be friends. "So, tell me everything that happened after Clyde hit me with his gun."

Lucas darted a glance at her and frowned. "We don't need to go into that right now."

"Yes, we do. I want to know." Her head was starting to ache, in spite of the pain reliever the hospital had given her, and she felt exhausted and frightened and perilously near the end of her rope. "I'm paying you to work for me, and I want a full report on what happened at my house this afternoon."

He gave a short gasp and then glanced at her, a scowl etched across his features. "Excuse me, Mrs. Lockhart, I guess I forgot for a moment that I'm only the hired help instead of a friend who's concerned about how you're feeling. I won't make that mistake again."

Her throat constricted at the harsh tone of his words, but she couldn't let him know how much she regretted what she'd said. Putting a little more distance between them was for the best, even if it hurt to see him scowl at her like that. "Then, please, tell me what I want to know."

His lips pursed for a moment, and then he began to speak. As the description of what had happened while she was unconscious began to unfold, she found her heart rate accelerating. When he described falling to the ground and shielding her with his body, she began to tremble. When he'd finished, she had the urge to reach over and squeeze his arm, but she forced her hands to remain in her lap.

"Thank you for saving my life."

"You're welcome. Just part of the job." His clipped tone pierced her heart, and she groaned inwardly. He didn't look at her but stared through the windshield, the muscle in his jaw flexing.

She swallowed hard and turned her head to stare out the window of the car. Ten minutes later they pulled into the driveway at his parents' home. She was out of the car and walking toward the porch before he caught up with her. The front door opened immediately, and Mrs. Knight stood there, a worried expression on her face.

"I thought you would never get here." She reached for Mia's arm and pulled her inside and underneath the entry hall light. "Lucas told me you were hurt. Let me get a look at your head."

Mia smiled. "I'm okay. No need to fuss."

Mrs. Knight checked the bandage on the wound and nodded. "It seems good to me, but I'll keep a close watch on you tonight."

Lucas stepped into the house and headed for the stairs. For the first time Mia noticed that he had her suitcase in his hand. Her eyes widened in surprise. "Where did that come from?"

He stopped on the first step and glanced around at her. "I went back in the house and gathered up some of your clothes before I came to the hospital. That's what we went there to get. So I'll take this up to your bedroom, and then I'll go on home," he said.

"You'll do nothing of the kind," his mother replied. "You're staying for dinner."

Lucas shook his head. "I can't, Mom. I'm tired, and I want to get on home."

"But I made your favorite, spaghetti. You can leave as soon as you've eaten."

"Mom, please." He sighed and shook his head. "Not tonight."

His mother's eyes darkened, and she bit down on her lip. "All right, darling. If that's what you want."

The atmosphere seemed charged with electricity, and Mia darted a glance at Mrs. Knight. "Can I help you get dinner ready?"

Mrs. Knight pulled her gaze away from her son and reached out to squeeze Mia's hand. "After what you've gone through today, absolutely not. Now, go sit down in the den until I get the food on the table."

Mia cast a quick glance at Lucas, who had continued upstairs, and headed toward him. "I think I'll go see what Lucas packed in my suitcase."

Without waiting for a reply, Mia hurried to the steps and arrived at the bedroom just as Lucas set down her suitcase. He pressed his hands on top of the case, bowed his head and exhaled a deep breath. When he straightened and turned around, his eyes grew wide. His gaze traveled over her face as he stared at her standing in the doorway.

"I didn't know you had followed me upstairs." He took a step toward her. "Do you need any help unpacking?"

She shook her head. "Lucas, I think I insulted you in the car, and I wanted to apologize."

He arched an eyebrow. "Oh? Could you possibly be talking about what you said about me being the hired help who was supposed to report to you?"

Tears filled her eyes. "I didn't mean it to sound like that, Lucas. I just don't know how to act with you. When I came to see you, at first you acted like I was the enemy. You've made it clear that you would like for us to try to be friends, but I think it's fair to say that neither of us knows if that's possible. Then today I wake up, and you're kissing my forehead. It's hard to understand."

He raked his hand through his hair and nodded. "We were in love once, Mia. And you're right, I don't know if we can ever be friends or not. It's like we take one step forward, and then two back. But I think if we work at it, we can have some kind of relationship."

Tears blurred her vision. "I think so, too. I'll try."

"I'm really not in the mood to talk about it tonight. I'll see you in the morning."

Mia nodded and moved aside as he walked from the room. She closed the door behind him and leaned against it a moment. Then, shaking her head, she walked over and lifted the lid of the suitcase, her eyes opening in surprise.

Teddy lay on top of her clothes, his one eye staring up at her. She picked him up and held him close as she sank down on the bed. Today Lucas had saved her life, and then he'd gone back into the house and brought her the one thing that he knew would bring comfort to her.

Tears began to roll down her cheeks. She'd taken Lucas's kindness for granted years ago. Now, after the years of abuse she had suffered at Kyle's hands, she could appreciate all those times he'd insisted on staying late at night at her rehearsals so he could walk her back across a dark campus. How he'd dragged her away from cramming for exams to make sure she had a healthy meal. And how he'd always shown up with her favorites—strawberry ice cream and a chocolate cupcake—when she was sad because her father had ignored her birthday.

And she'd repaid him by breaking his heart. She took a deep breath, stood up and placed Teddy on the table beside the bed.

She should never have come to him for help. It could only remind him of her betrayal. After all these years, she'd shown up with all the baggage her choices had made, and she wasn't going to make Lucas suffer any more than he already had. As soon as Tony Chapman was behind bars, she would be on her way. Then Lucas would never have to see her again.

* * *

Lucas slammed on the car's brakes just in time to keep from running through a red light. Behind him horns blared as vehicles slid to a stop in the heavy morning commuter traffic. His face burned with embarrassment that he'd let his thoughts distract him. That wasn't like him at all.

He rubbed his fingers across his eyes and sighed. Even after two cups of coffee and several aspirins this morning, his head still pounded as if a marching band had taken up residence inside. That wasn't surprising after the sleepless night he'd had. Every time he'd closed his eyes, the memory of his arms around Mia's still body returned to taunt him.

That vision had then been quickly replaced by her words later. *I'm paying you to work for me*, she'd said, and his heart had shriveled at the icy tone of her voice.

How could he have been so foolish? He'd let down his guard and had acknowledged the feelings he still had for her. He'd even wondered if he was ready to trust her again, to let go of the doubts that lingered from their past. She had put a stop to that. She'd made it perfectly clear that she wanted nothing from him except his services as a bounty hunter, and he'd do well to remember that.

A car horn blared at him, jarring him from his thoughts, and he jerked to attention. The traffic light had turned green. With an apologetic wave, he stepped on the accelerator and drove forward.

Ten minutes later he stepped onto the front porch of his parents' home and took a deep breath. Professional facade, that's what he hoped he could maintain today. No talk of friendship. Nothing that could be construed as personal. Just another client with the Knight Fugitive Recovery Agency. That's all Mia was.

He pushed the front door open, stopped inside the entry and inhaled. The aroma of cinnamon and cloves drifted through the house, and he closed his eyes as his stomach rumbled. His mother was baking this morning, and the smell reminded him of the mornings right before Christmas when he was a child and would wake to the smell of his mother's holiday spice cake drifting through the house. He licked his lips in anticipation of devouring a big piece of the cake with its thick buttercream frosting.

He headed to the kitchen and stopped at the door as he spotted his mother and Mia sitting at the table having a cup of coffee. His mother turned and smiled when she heard him at the door. "Lucas, I didn't expect you this early. I was just changing the bandage on Mia's head."

"And how does it look?"

His mother turned back to the table and picked up the emergency first-aid kit that she'd been using ever since he could remember. "Everything seems to be good this morning. Why don't you sit down and have some coffee while I put this away?"

He shook his head. "I've already had some, but I would take a slice of that cake." He grinned, knowing what her answer would be.

"That cake is for the Christmas bazaar at the church. I'm taking it with me when we go to church this morning. If you want a piece, you'll have to go by there tomorrow and buy it."

"Aw, Mom," he whined. "I'll pay you for it right now."

Her eyes sparkled, and she shook her head. "Don't worry. I'll bake another cake for Christmas dinner, and you'd better be here to help eat it."

Lucas arched his eyebrows and kissed her on the cheek. "And where else would I be but here with my family that day?"

His mother laughed and patted him on the cheek. "You'd better be, if you know what's good for you." She smiled down at Mia who as yet hadn't spoken to him. "And what about you, Mia? Can you join us for Christmas dinner?"

Mia's face flushed, and she shook her head as she reached for her coffee cup. "I don't think so. I'm sure Lucas will have tracked Tony down by that time, and I'll be gone."

His mother frowned. "Christmas is only a week away. I hope Tony is back in jail by that time, but you're welcome to join us whether he's caught or not."

"Thank you. We'll see what happens."

Taking a deep breath, Lucas's mother glanced at Mia before she checked her watch. "Oh, Lucas, I didn't know it was getting so late. After church your father and I are having lunch at the mall and then finishing our Christmas shopping. Are you and Mia coming to church?"

Mia didn't look up at him, and he raked his hand through his hair. "I don't know. I thought you might be home after church, but I guess I can take her with me again. She has to have a bodyguard."

"Good," his mother said as she hurried to the coatrack next to the back door. "I'll see you two later. Have a nice day."

When his mother was gone, Lucas walked to the counter, poured himself a cup of coffee and sat down at the table. Mia didn't glance up but wrapped her fingers around her mug and stared down into its contents.

After a minute she straightened her shoulders and looked up at Lucas. The bandage on the side of her head wrinkled as she frowned at him. "I don't need a babysitter."

Lucas took a sip of coffee before he answered. "I never said you did."

"Having to take me with you sounds like an imposition. Why can't I just stay here?"

Lucas exhaled. "I don't think it's safe for you to be alone, not until I've found Chapman."

Mia was silent for a moment before she spoke. "Lucas, I know you don't take other clients with you when you're tracking a fugitive. I don't want any special treatment from you. Just find Tony Chapman. Then I'll go away, and you'll never have to deal with me again."

Her words sliced back through the wound her statement last night had left, and Lucas pushed back from the table. Gritting his teeth, he stood and strode toward the living room but stopped before he exited the kitchen. Slowly he turned and came back to where she still sat at the table. She stared up at him, and a slight tremor pulled at the corner of her mouth.

"Mia, I get the message. It was loud and clear

yesterday, and now you've repeated it. But you don't have to worry. I understand how you feel about me. I'd hoped we could be friends, but I don't think that's going to be possible now."

A startled look flashed across her face, and she stared up at him. "What message? What are you talking about?"

He closed his eyes for a moment and bit down on his lip. Why was he doing this now? He needed to let it alone, but his heart told him to be honest. "I know you have hard feelings about how I deserted you, and I'm sorry about that. I was wrong to do it."

Her mouth dropped open, and she frowned. "Deserted me? I don't understand."

"If I had done things differently, you never would have had to go through what you suffered with Kyle. I'm sorry I let you down."

Mia pushed to her feet and shook her head. "You didn't…"

Lucas held up his hand to stop her. "I did. When I asked you to put our wedding off because I wanted to pursue my own dream of being a navy SEAL, I didn't give a thought to how you'd feel about that decision. I knew you'd always felt abandoned by your father, and yet there I was—abandoning you, too. I ignored everything you wanted and left you with no other choice than to go back to your father's house—a place where you'd always been so unhappy. If I had taken care of you, you never would have met Kyle, and things would have turned out differently. I'm sorry you've suffered because of me."

Mia reached out and grasped his arm. "Lucas, you can't blame yourself for the mistakes I made. If I'd been strong enough, I never would have given in to my father's pressure to marry Kyle. But I didn't know what else to do. I hadn't heard from you, and I thought you'd moved on."

"Not heard from me?" he almost yelled. "I emailed, but every one I sent bounced back that the address wasn't valid. I tried calling, but your number was no longer in service. Then I resorted to writing letter after letter, but I never heard a word in reply from you. And yet when I came home a year later, I still went to your father's house to find you, but a maid told me you were married and no longer living at home."

Her eyes had grown large while he talked. Finally, she said, "I was so angry at you when I had to go back home that I changed my email address and got a new phone. But I never received any letters."

"Well, I sent them. Maybe somebody at your father's house didn't want you to get them."

"That's possible. I know my father wanted me to move past my feelings for you, especially once I met Kyle at a charity fund-raiser. Kyle set off from the start to sweep me off my feet, and I was ready to have some attention from a man. We were married a few months later. It didn't take me long to realize what a mistake I'd made. I'd thrown away whatever chance I might have had with you. Now it's too late."

Lucas's hands curled into fists at his side. "Mia, please, don't say that. I thought we were going to try and be friends."

She shook her head. "We can't, Lucas. Too much happened in the past. I'm not the same person I was when we were in college. I'm too damaged, and you deserve better than having a friend like me. I'll be fine on my own, once this situation is resolved. All I need is to have some peace in my life, but I can't do that until Tony is back in jail."

Lucas rubbed the back of his neck and pursed his lips. Well, if that's what she wanted, he'd better get busy trying to give it to her. Because being around her was dredging up too many old feelings, and he couldn't take much more.

He gave a curt nod. "Then we're wasting time talking when we could be looking for him. And I said *we* because there's no way I can leave you here alone. You're right that I wouldn't take another client along, but this is a special case. Not only am I trying to find Chapman for you, but I need to protect you from him, too. So get your coat and let's head out."

Mia took a deep breath. "Okay. Thank you again for helping me, and I promise to try and not put either of us in danger today. Where are we going?"

"I have several places I'd like to visit. From what the police told me yesterday, I suspect that Kyle was involved in smuggling items into the country and maybe out to foreign places, too." He glanced at his watch. "I checked Shackleford's website this morning, and they open at noon on Sunday. I want to go there and see if we can find out anything. If Kyle and Chapman were working together, maybe somebody there knows something. Why don't we go to church with my folks, then we can drive downtown to Shackleford's and be there when they open?"

"That sounds like a good idea. But you said you had several places you want to visit. Where else, besides Shackleford's?"

He took a deep breath. "I'd like to talk to Christine Abbott. The boat Clyde used came from her dock, and she seemed to have some kind of relationship with Kyle."

Mia's eyes grew wide, and her face paled. "Relationship? Do you mean like in having an affair?"

Lucas shrugged. "I don't know. But their pictures seemed to show up together in the paper a lot."

She swallowed, and he watched the muscles in her throat constrict. "So he couldn't be faithful to that part of his marriage vows either."

Lucas's heart lurched at the flash of sorrow on her face. "I don't know, Mia. It's just a suspicion, but there was some kind of connection between them."

She tossed her head back, and her hair swept across the side of her face. "Well, let's go find out. I'll get my coat."

He closed his eyes and shook his head as she strode from the kitchen. He hadn't wanted to have a heart-to-heart talk this morning, but maybe it was best. Now he knew how she felt, and she sure didn't want to renew any kind of relationship with him. The feelings for her that had resurfaced were just going to have to be ignored.

His head might know that, but making his heart understand was an entirely different matter. With a sigh he walked to the front door and waited for her to come downstairs.

NINE

Mia had been silent ever since they left church. Now as Lucas drove toward the downtown area, he glanced at her out of the corner of his eye. "How did you enjoy the service?"

She turned to him and smiled. "I thought it was wonderful. It's been a long time since I was in church on Sunday, and I realized how much I've missed it. When I get settled after this is all over, I'm going to find a church and get involved."

Lucas nodded. "That sounds like a good idea. The people at our church are like extended family. They're the kind of folks you want to have around when trouble comes into your life."

"I could tell. Everybody was so friendly. And it was good to see Adam, meet his wife and see Jessica. I was sorry Ryan wasn't there. I really liked him when I met him. You're a very lucky man, Lucas, to have such a great family."

"I am," he said. He glanced at her, but she had turned her head and was staring out the window.

Neither one of them spoke again until he pulled the car to a stop across the street from Shackleford's Imports. She gazed at the building, frowning. He'd seen that look before, and he knew she was frightened, wondering what lay behind the doors of the place where her husband had worked.

He studied the buildings up and down the street. They were older, dating back to Memphis's heyday, when it was a booming riverfront town. Now renovated and given expensive face-lifts, these hallmarks of the past occupied some of the most expensive property in the city.

Shackleford's was no exception. An awning hung over the double glass doors that led inside, and elegant antique furniture sat showcased in large windows on either side of the entryway. Crystal chandeliers cast a bright glow over the merchandise on display. Lucas gave a low whistle as his gaze drifted over the front of the business.

"This place sure looks fancy," he said.

Mia nodded. "It is. The pieces for sale here aren't for anyone on a budget. Kyle worked here for seven years, and yet I was never in this place over two or three times. It seems strange to be coming here now."

Lucas swiveled in his seat to look at her. "And you don't know anyone who works here?"

"No. I met Mr. Shackleford when Kyle first joined the staff, but he's been ill and hasn't been too involved in the running of the place for the past few years. From what I gathered, Kyle had been in charge since Mr. Shackleford had to take a leave of absence. Kyle would report to him and let him know how things were going, but he never came to the business."

Lucas opened the car door. "Let's go see who's here today."

When they passed through the double doors, Lucas felt as if he'd stepped back in history. Although he'd never studied antiques, he knew the items scattered across the showroom floor and the paintings hanging on the walls were much rarer and pricier than any of the modern home furnishings one might find in a local retail store.

Every piece of furniture in the place glowed with a patina that could only be produced by aging and delicate care. As they walked along an aisle that ran through the middle of the showroom, he tried to take it all in, but it was difficult to see everything.

They passed several cases that held antique jewelry, and his gaze landed on a cameo brooch much like one he remembered his grandmother wearing. He hesitated for a moment to get a better look, and a voice sounded nearby.

"Good morning. Is there something I can help you with today?"

Lucas turned to see a woman who looked to be about thirty years old standing nearby. The black dress and the diamond earrings with a matching pendant she wore gave off the same quality of elegance that the showroom displayed.

Lucas smiled, touched Mia's elbow and ushered her closer to the woman. "My name is Lucas Knight, and this is my friend Mia Lockhart, Kyle Lockhart's widow. I don't know if you're aware of it or not, but the man charged with murdering Mrs. Lockhart's husband has jumped bail. I'm a bounty hunter, and Mrs. Lockhart has hired me to help track him down. I wonder if you might be able to help us."

The woman's pencil-thin eyebrows pulled down, and a look of sympathy shaded her eyes. "Oh, Mrs. Lockhart, I'm Janet Williams. I'm sorry I didn't recognize you. I saw you at Mr. Lockhart's funeral. I can't tell you how sorry I am for your loss."

"Thank you, Janet. I'm afraid I don't remember much about that day," Mia said.

Janet turned back to Lucas. "I don't know how I could help you. I didn't know the man who was arrested."

"We really didn't expect that you would. What we're really interested in finding out is whether or not Kyle had a business connection of some kind to him. Did you ever hear Kyle mention the name Tony Chapman?"

Janet shook her head. "No."

"What about Clyde Harper?"

"I've never heard of him either," she said.

Lucas thought for a moment before he spoke again. "And you would have known about Mr. Lockhart's business contacts because you worked with him directly, right? What exactly is your job, Janet?"

She gave a short laugh and shrugged. "It depends on what needs to be done. Up until Mr. Shackleford got sick, I was in charge of acquiring items to sell and of working with special clients who had a specific piece in mind."

Lucas wrinkled his forehead and nodded. "That sounds like a very important position. But you said you did that *before* Mr. Shackleford got sick."

"Yes. When he became ill, he appointed

Mr. Lockhart to manage the business, and Mr. Lockhart decided he wanted to have full control over acquisitions. I took over the marketing of the business and became a salesperson on the showroom floor."

Mia, who'd been listening mutely, suddenly spoke up. "That sounds like a demotion. Did Kyle explain why he wanted to change your responsibilities?"

"We had begun to deal in antiquities more, and he said he understood that market better than I did. He also thought it better if a man traveled to some of the places where these treasures were available." She frowned as she said it, and Lucas was quick to follow up on the discontent in her expression.

"You didn't agree with him?" he asked.

She shrugged, looking embarrassed. "Since the internet had become our chief way of tracking down items for sale, I wasn't convinced the travel he did was necessary. But he was the boss, and I needed my job."

Lucas was about to ask another question when a door at the side of the showroom opened, and a man pushing a cart loaded with cleaning supplies entered the room. Janet glanced over her shoulder at him. "Donnie," she called out, "what are you doing with that cart? The custodian should be here any time now."

Donnie chuckled and shook his head. "I knew he was running late today. I thought I'd help him out a bit."

With a nod in their direction he disappeared through a door in the back of the showroom, and Janet turned her attention back to Lucas and Mia. "That's Donnie Miller," she said. "Mr. Lockhart hired him as our shipping and receiving clerk."

Lucas stared at the door that Donnie had entered and frowned as he remembered Clyde's mention of smuggling. He glanced back at Janet. "I suppose you have items arriving and being shipped out all the time."

Janet nodded. "That's right. We import and export items regularly."

"Who keeps a record of all the transactions?"

"That was my job when Mr. Shackleford was here, but when Mr. Lockhart took over, he hired Donnie to do that. He keeps records on the computer of all items received and shipped. But we've had a difficult time since Mr. Lockhart's death."

"And why's that?"

A shadow of a frown crossed her face. "When Mr. Lockhart's body was found in his office, we discovered there were quite a few items stolen. Among them were the three computers we used to keep our records, as well as the external hard drives where we backed up all our information. Donnie and I are in the process of doing an inventory of the business, but it's going to take some time. At this point we really don't know what antiques the thieves might have taken."

"Don't you have hard copies of invoices of items bought?"

Janet hesitated before she answered. "We did, but the files that had anything to do with acquisitions and sales were taken from Mr. Lockhart's office after the murder. I know at first the police thought his death was a robbery gone wrong, but I think they may have changed their minds after they discovered the missing files. Why would a thief want file folders filled with purchase orders and receipts?"

"That's a good question," Lucas said. "And one I don't have the answer for. Is there anything else you can tell us about the murder that might be of help?"

Janet bit down on her lip and glanced over her shoulder as if checking to see if anyone was listening. "There is one more thing, something that's been troubling me."

Lucas frowned. "What is it?"

Janet took a deep breath, stepped closer and lowered her voice. "The day before Mr. Lockhart was killed I came back after dinner to finish a marketing campaign I was working on, and I saw the light on in his office. His door was slightly ajar, and I walked over to tell him I was back in the building. I stopped when I heard him talking to someone."

"Did you know who was in there with him?" Lucas asked.

"Oh, yes. I recognized the voice right away. It was Ms. Abbott, one of our top customers." She glanced at Mia, and she bit down on her lip as if she didn't know whether or not to go on.

"And?" Lucas prompted.

After a moment Janet continued. "Through the crack in the door I could see a large leather pouch on the desk, and Mr. Lockhart was about to open it. I know I should have backed away, but for some reason, I couldn't. I wanted to see what was in that pouch."

"And did you?"

Janet nodded. "Mr. Lockhart reached in, and he pulled out a woman's ring. Not one with any kind of gems in it, but just a plain gold ring. He held it up to the light and smiled, then scooped a large handful of jewelry and coins from the bag and spread his fingers as it tumbled back into the pouch. It reminded me of a pirate sifting through a chest of treasure. Just when I thought that was probably all of it, he pulled out what looked like a large amulet hanging on a leather thong. He handed it to Ms. Abbott, and she held it up to her neck. 'How do I look?' she asked. 'Like a ten-million-dollar Roman goddess,' Mr. Lockhart responded.''

Lucas cast a quick glance at Mia. Her eyes had grown wide, and her lips trembled. His stomach roiled at the look of despair on her face. He could see that she thought this was proof that her husband had been cheating on her after all. Was it possible that in spite of everything he'd done to her, she had loved Kyle Lockhart? And had the insinuation that there had been something between him and Christine Abbott been too much for her to bear? Before he could say anything, she turned to stare across the showroom at a brocade sofa. Her chin trembled, and she balled her hands into fists as if she was trying to gain control of her tense body. After a moment she took a deep breath and turned back to him.

Lucas took a step closer to her. "Mia, are you okay?"

She lifted her chin and nodded. "I'm fine." Her throaty rasp made his heart prick.

He frowned as he turned back to Janet and cleared his throat. "Roman goddess? What did you make of that?"

Janet shrugged. "I thought maybe he was showing her a new acquisition, but I didn't know how in the world he'd come up with the money to purchase that jewelry for the store if it really was worth ten million dollars. When I was keeping records, we never had those kinds of funds to invest in artifacts. And I knew those pieces had to be artifacts. I'd seen some very much like them once in a museum in Italy. They looked like they might have been from the Roman period."

Lucas did the math in his head and gave a low whistle. "Then that would make them something like two thousand years old or more."

"Yes, and very valuable."

A soft gasp escaped Mia's lips. "Where's the jewelry now?"

"I have no idea," Janet said. "But I've been thinking about what they said next, and it doesn't make any sense to me."

Lucas tilted his head to one side and inched closer to Janet. "What did they say?"

Janet licked her lips and frowned as if trying to recall their words. "I don't remember exactly how they said it, but Ms. Abbott asked Mr. Lockhart where he was going to put it to keep it away from the others until they left to go see the buyer. And he responded that he'd been thinking about that. He said he couldn't put it in the safe because that was the first place they'd look, but he had come up with a place they'd never suspect."

Lucas's pulse rate had increased with each word Janet had spoken. "And where was that?"

Janet shrugged. "He said he was going to hide it in plain sight. At that point I decided I'd better get out of there, and I left without letting them see me. Mr. Lockhart didn't say anything about the jewelry the next day, and then he was killed that night. I decided the pouch must have been stolen in the robbery."

"Have you told the police about this?" Lucas asked.

"Yes, I told them everything I've told you. But I've been thinking about that jewelry, and I'd like to know more about it. I know a curator at a museum in London who's an expert in Roman antiquities. I emailed him yesterday afternoon before I left for the day and described what I saw. I asked him to let me know if he had any idea who Mr. Lockhart could have purchased that lot from."

"And have you heard from him?"

Janet shook her head and glanced down at her watch. "With the difference in the time, it would have been eleven o'clock at night there when I sent the message, and he would have been at home. It's late afternoon there now, and I thought I would have heard from him by this time, but nothing yet. Of course he may be doing some research for me."

Lucas pulled one of his cards from his pocket and handed it to Janet. "All my information is on this. If you hear from him, I'd appreciate you letting me know what he says."

She took the card and stuck it in her pocket. "I'll be glad to, Mr. Knight. Is there anything else I can do for you today?"

Lucas glanced toward the door that Donnie Miller had entered a few minutes ago. "Do you mind if I talk with Mr. Miller before we leave?"

She shook her head. "No, I'll take you back there."

Lucas and Mia followed as she led them to the back of the showroom where she opened the door and called out, "Donnie, there are some people here who would like to talk with you." Before the man could answer, a chime sounded from the front of the store, and Janet glanced in that direction. "A customer just came in. I need to see if she needs some help."

Donnie Miller appeared at that moment, his gaze darting from Lucas to Mia. A puzzled look flashed across his face, and he puffed out a short breath. "You want to talk to me?" he asked as Janet hurried away.

Lucas held out his hand as he made introductions, and Donnie's eyes darkened at the mention of Mia's name. "I was sorry to hear about Mr. Lockhart. He was very good to me. He gave me a job when I needed one."

"Thank you," Mia murmured.

He directed his attention back to Lucas. "How can I help you?"

"Ms. Williams tells me that you are responsible for receiving any acquisitions that are delivered to the business."

He nodded. "That's right."

"Do you remember receiving a shipment that included some gold jewelry, maybe pieces made during the time of the Roman empire?"

Donnie frowned and shook his head. "No. Ms. Williams has already asked me about that, and I told her I never saw a shipment like that."

"Did you ever hear Mr. Lockhart mention

any pieces from that era? Could they possibly have been delivered directly to him?"

Donnie shook his head. "He never said anything to me, and he wasn't in the habit of accepting deliveries." His eyebrows pulled into a frown. "What's this all about? Why such an interest in some jewelry all of a sudden?"

Lucas shrugged. "Just trying to make sense out of Kyle Lockhart's murder." He pulled another card from his pocket and handed it to Donnie. "If you think of anything that might help us get to the bottom of why he was killed, get in touch with me."

Donnie looked down at the card and slipped it in his pocket before he nodded. "Okay, but I've told you and the police I don't know anything that might help. The night Mr. Lockhart was killed, I had left work early because I had tickets to a Predators game in Nashville. I ended up spending the night there and driving back home early the next morning."

"I see," Lucas said. "Like I said, if you think of anything else. Thanks for talking to us." He turned to leave but stopped and faced Donnie. "One more thing, did you ever meet a man named Tony Chapman?"

Donnie frowned. "That's the name of the

man the police arrested for Mr. Lockhart's murder, isn't it?"

"Yes. Chapman's DNA was on file because he'd been in prison, and they found it in the skin particles under Lockhart's fingernails."

Donnie nodded. "I read that in the paper, but I'd never heard of him then."

"What about Clyde Harper?"

Donnie shook his head again. "Never heard of him either."

"Okay, thanks for talking to us today," Lucas said as he grabbed Mia's arm and steered her toward the door. As they walked back through the showroom, she pulled free of his grasp, and Lucas let his hand drift down to his side. Once outside, she stopped and stared across the street where he'd parked the car.

Lucas inched closer to her. "Are you okay, Mia?"

She bit down on her lip and nodded. "Yeah. Hearing Janet talk made me realize how little I knew about Kyle." She turned to him and gave a wobbly smile. "But don't worry about me. I'll be all right."

Before he could respond, she turned and strode toward his car. He followed a few feet behind her. When she was about halfway to the vehicle, Lucas looked around in surprise at the roar of an SUV that had just rounded the corner and was headed straight toward Mia.

"Mia!" he yelled at the top of his voice, and she stopped to look back at him.

His heart pounded like a jackhammer as he sprinted toward her. A look of fear crossed her face just as he reached out and grabbed her around the waist. Their bodies sailed through the air and skidded to a stop on the ground next to the car, his body covering hers. He heard a gunshot and felt the shattered glass from the car window rain down on him before he blacked out.

One minute Mia was standing in the middle of the street. The next, Lucas plowed into her like a defensive lineman, and she hit the pavement with Lucas's weight on top of her. Now shards of glass were scattered near her, and she lay still for a moment trying to remember what had happened. Then it came back to her. The roar of a car, Lucas tackling her and the pavement coming up to meet her.

She tried to push up, but she couldn't budge Lucas. "Lucas," she moaned. "Are you okay?"

When he didn't answer, she worked her arm free from underneath her body and reached up to touch his head. Her hand came away sticky and red with his blood. A scream tore from her throat, and then she felt his body being moved off her.

"Are you all right?" a voice shrieked. Mia turned her head slightly to see Janet Williams leaning over her.

"Lucas," she gasped. "Is *he* all right?"

At that moment his body twitched, and he jerked his eyes open. "Mia?" his groggy voice rasped. "Are you hurt?"

"We've called 911. They'll be here in a few minutes. Can you get up?" Mia recognized the frightened voice of Donnie Miller.

Lucas pushed into a sitting position, and Mia sat up beside him. Her eyes grew wide at the blood that oozed from the cut above his eyebrow. "Lucas, you're injured," she cried.

He shook his head. "No, I blacked out for a minute, but I'm fine." He touched the cut above his eye and winced. "I must have gotten hit by a flying piece of glass."

Mia started to respond, but the sound of sirens split the air. She glanced over her shoulder to see a police car followed by an ambulance speeding toward them. They came to an abrupt stop beside them, and Janet and Donnie stepped out of the way as two EMTs ran toward them. Within seconds Lucas and Mia were both being examined.

Mia tried to concentrate on the questions an EMT named Eli was asking her, but she was too concerned about Lucas. She heard the attendant examining him say that he could find no broken bones, and she sighed in relief. Minutes later Lucas, a bandage covering the cut above his eye, pushed to his feet and turned to one of the police officers. As he began to relate what had happened, she directed her attention back to Eli, who now was applying a fresh dressing to the cut on her head where Clyde had hit her.

"How did you get this injury?" Eli asked.

"Uh, a guy tried to kidnap me yesterday and hit me in the head with a gun," she mumbled.

His eyes grew wide. "Kidnap you? And today a car almost kills you. Sounds like you have somebody after you."

She gave a weak smile. "I guess you could say that."

She stared down at the ground and took hold of Eli's hand as he pulled her to her feet. "Steady now," he said. "Hold on to me until you feel like you can stand alone."

She released his hand and nodded. "Thank you, but I'm okay."

"Are you sure?" Lucas appeared at her side, concern lining his face.

"I'm okay, Lucas. How about you?"

He pointed to the bandage above his eye. "Just a scratch. No stitches required."

Eli chuckled and put his hands on his hips as he took in the bandages Lucas and Mia wore. "From the looks of things, I don't think you two can stay out of trouble."

Mia glanced at Lucas and burst into laughter. "I think Mr. Knight is wishing about now that he'd never agreed to take me as a client," she said.

Lucas's face turned red as he tried to control the embarrassed grin pulling at his mouth, but it was the look in his eyes that caused her pulse to race. "You're wrong, Mia. I'd hate to think of you facing all of this alone. I'm glad you showed up on my doorstep."

"I am, too." Mia smiled and nodded.

Thirty minutes later, with the police report finished and Mia and Lucas having assured the EMTs that they didn't need to go to the hospital, they drove away from the scene of the shooting. The wind blew through the shattered window, and Lucas turned the heater up higher. Even with the increased heat, Mia still shivered. Lucas glanced at Mia and caught sight of her hunched shoulders inside her coat. "I know you're cold. Mom should be home soon. Do you want to go back and stay with her this afternoon?"

Mia's eyebrows arched. "Why? What are you planning on doing?"

"I thought I'd go see Christine Abbott. I can understand why that might be uncomfortable for you. So I'll drop you off at my parents' house if you'd rather stay there."

She shook her head. "No way. I want to meet this woman who seemed to know my husband so well. But I would like to ride in comfort. Why don't we take your car to your house and get mine? At least it has windows."

He laughed and nodded. "That sounds good. Then I'll take you for lunch. I think after your two close calls, you deserve something special. How about stopping at that rib place that we liked so much when we were in college?"

Tears pooled in her eyes, and she turned her head to stare out the window to keep him from seeing them. Her throat constricted, almost making it impossible to respond. Finally she swallowed and swiveled to face him as she forced herself to speak. "Thank you, Lucas," she whispered.

His eyebrows arched, and he darted a glance at her. "For what?"

"For being so kind to me. I've thought of that restaurant so many times over the years and wished I could go there again. But of course that wasn't possible. Now you offer to take me." His hand rested on the gear shift, and she covered it with hers. "I've never brought you anything but problems, but you still find ways to make me feel special. You are the best person I've ever known."

His Adam's apple bobbed as he glanced down at her hand, then he slid his from the gear shift and wrapped it around hers. She closed her eyes at the way her heart pounded at the feel of her fingers in his warm palm.

"No, I'm not, but I'm glad you think so."

She lay back against the headrest and closed her eyes as they drove through the Memphis streets, their fingers laced together. It had been a long time since she'd felt so peaceful, and she wanted to savor every minute of it.

Two hours later Mia almost wished she'd asked Lucas to take her to his parents' house. Toasty warm from the heat pouring through the vents of her car and feeling stuffed from the half rack of ribs she'd eaten, all Mia wanted was to lie down and take a long nap.

Instead here she and Lucas were pulling to a stop in the circle driveway of Christine Abbott's house. Mia's breath hitched in her throat at the thought that the house of horrors she had shared with Kyle lay just on the other side of the wooded area next to the Abbott property. The memory of the boat Clyde Harper had tried to abduct her in flashed in her mind. The dock behind Christine's house wasn't visible from the front, but Mia's stomach still roiled at the thought that Clyde's boat had come from here. But had it been stolen or borrowed? That was the question. And Christine Abbott had the answers to that as well as other things Mia would like to know about.

She shook her head to rid it of the thought of Kyle being involved with Christine. But why should it surprise her? He'd only married her because he wanted the prestige and contacts that came with her father's wealth. Kyle and her father had been two of a kind, both self-centered and oblivious to the needs of anyone else. Neither one had ever loved her, and she'd accepted that years ago.

Next to her Lucas turned off the engine, and she studied his profile. A soft stubble covered his jawline, and she longed to run her fingers over it like she'd done years ago. But that was then, before she had made her biggest mistake and cut him out of her life. If only she could go back and redo the past. But that was impossible.

Lucas glanced around at her. "Are you ready?"

She took a deep breath and nodded. "As I'll ever be."

They climbed out of the car and walked together toward the rambling two-story white colonial house with its six columns across the front. This house was much bigger than the one she'd lived in, but just being in this neighborhood made her stomach churn.

Lucas placed his hand on her elbow as they walked up the wide brick steps and headed toward the double doors decorated with large Christmas wreaths of holly and red berries. When they stopped at the doorway, Mia reached out to ring the bell, but Lucas grabbed her hand.

"Wait!"

She flinched at the urgency in his voice and whirled to face him. "What's wrong?"

He pointed to the door. "It's open."

Mia looked where he indicated and sucked in her breath at the sight of the door ajar. But that wasn't the only thing that made her heart beat like a bass drum. Dried brownish-red droplets were spattered up and down the side of the door.

Mia gasped and pointed a shaking finger at the spots. "I-is that bl-blood?"

Lucas's mouth settled into a grim line, and he nodded as he pulled his gun from his holster. Then he grasped Mia's arm and pulled her behind him. "Stay back," he whispered.

He placed the toe of his boot against the bottom of the door and nudged it forward. A soft creaking sound drifted up as the door swung inward and then thumped against the wall. Lucas gasped, and Mia peeped around his side to get a glimpse of what he'd seen.

Her eyes grew wide, and she jammed her fist against her lips to keep from screaming. A woman, her blond hair soaked with blood, lay in the entry of the mansion.

"It looks like someone didn't want us to talk to Christine Abbott," Lucas said.

Mia looked once more at the still body and then ran to the edge of the porch, leaned over and proceeded to lose all the ribs she'd eaten earlier.

TEN

As soon as he'd viewed the body, Lucas had recognized Christine Abbott from the pictures of her with Kyle Lockhart. He'd seen enough death when he was a navy SEAL to know that she'd been dead for some time.

"I-is that Christine Abbott?" Mia whispered when she returned to his side.

He settled his mouth in a grim line and nodded. "Yeah."

"What do we do?"

Lucas pulled his cell phone from his pocket. "We call this in to the police, then we go to the car to wait for them to arrive."

"But don't we need to see if she needs help?"

He glanced over his shoulder at Mia. Her eyes held a glazed aspect, and it was if she couldn't look away from the scene in front of her. He took her by the hand, led her down the steps and opened the car door.

"Stay in here where it's warm until the police get here."

Mia's chest heaved with short gasps as she stared past him to the front door of the house. "But what if she's still alive? Maybe we can do something."

"Look at me, Mia," he ordered. She might have been deaf for the reaction his words had on her as she breathed heavily and gazed at the front door without blinking. Afraid that she was about to hyperventilate, Lucas grasped her chin with his fingers and directed her eyes to him. "Mia, I said look at me."

Her chin trembled, and he relaxed his hold a bit. She blinked and glanced up at him as if seeing him for the first time. "Lucas," she murmured.

"Listen to me," he said. "There's nothing we can do for Christine now, and we need to stay away from her body. If we go in, we may contaminate the crime scene, and that will only cause problems for the police. Now, please, get in the car and let me call this in."

She didn't move for a moment but then nodded. "Okay."

Without looking at the house again, she climbed in the car and closed the door. She crossed her arms over her chest and stared at him through the window as he punched 911 in his cell phone.

A dispatcher answered right away. "911. What is your emergency?"

"This is Lucas Knight. I'm at 567 Lakeshore Drive. I found the owner of the home dead in her entry. We need police and an ambulance."

"They're on their way, sir."

"Thank you."

He hung up and waited for the police. It was less than five minutes before he heard the sirens in the distance. Two police cars and an ambulance skidded to a stop in the driveway. One of the policemen ran toward him.

"Did you make the 911 call?"

Lucas nodded. "Yes. I'm Lucas Knight. When Ms. Lockhart and I arrived, I noticed the front door was ajar. After pushing it open, I saw Christine Abbot lying in the entry. I could tell she was dead, so I backed away and made the call. Didn't want to contaminate the crime scene."

"Thanks," he said. "We'll see what we can find." He glanced at the EMTs who were getting out of the ambulance and called out to them. "Let us check the house, guys, and I'll let you know when you can come in."

Lucas watched as the officers fanned out

around the building and began their search of the premises. Two of them entered the front door, and he could hear them discussing the condition of the house. From what he could tell, it had been ransacked just like Mia's.

Another car pulled into the driveway, and Lucas watched as Ryan and his partner, Mac Barnes, climbed from the car and stopped next to him. "Hey, Ryan. Jessica said you were working today. Did you guys get this case?" Lucas asked.

Ryan nodded. "Yeah. And I hear you made the 911 call. That right?"

Lucas tilted his head to one side and rubbed the back of his neck. "Yeah. The front door was ajar, and we spotted her in the entry."

Ryan's eyebrows arched. "We?"

The car door opened at that moment, and Mia stepped out. "Hi, Ryan."

Ryan's mouth gaped, and he turned to stare at Lucas. "You brought your client along on the hunt for Chapman?"

Lucas chuckled and shook his head. "I didn't have much choice—she needs protection around the clock. Chapman is determined to kill Mia. She's had several close calls, and then we get here and find the woman we want to question dead. Chapman would be at the top of my suspect list to be the murderer."

Mac frowned and glanced at Lucas. "I don't think I've met your client, Lucas. Why don't you introduce us?"

Mia turned to Lucas, and he nodded toward Mac. "Mia, this is Mac Barnes. He's Ryan's partner and worked with my sister, Jessica, too, when she was on the police force. Mac, this is Mia Lockhart, Kyle Lockhart's widow."

The lines in Mac's face deepened as he took Mia's hand in his. "I'm sorry about your husband, Mrs. Lockhart. We're doing everything we can to bring Tony Chapman to justice." He glanced at Lucas. "And if you have the Knight Agency helping you, I'm sure he'll be back behind bars in no time."

Mia smiled at Mac and squeezed his hand. "I'm looking forward to that."

He released Mia and turned to Lucas. "Want to give us your story before we go in and check the crime scene?"

Ryan and Mac both opened notebooks and began to write as Lucas recited the events that had taken place since he and Mia had driven up to the Abbott house. When he had finished, Mac looked back over his notes and pursed his lips. "And you didn't see anybody near the house when you arrived?"

Lucas shook his head. "No, and it appeared Ms. Abbott had been dead for some time."

Mac exhaled a deep breath and closed his notebook. "I guess that's all we need for now. If I have any questions, I know where to find you." He reached out and shook Lucas's hand. "Tell your folks and Adam and Claire hello for me." Then he smiled and turned to Mia. "And it was good meeting you, Mrs. Lockhart. Maybe we'll meet again soon."

"I hope so." She glanced from him to Ryan. "Good luck with the investigation."

"Thanks," he said with a smile and then turned to Lucas and slapped him on the back. "Seems like you've had your share of bad luck over the past few days. Try not to get yourself killed before Christmas. I'm looking forward to my first Christmas in the Knight family, and I'd hate to see you mess it up."

Lucas grinned and punched Ryan on the arm. "I knew I did the wrong thing when I told my sister to take a chance on you. Better watch your step. I still have a lot of influence over my twin."

Ryan and Mac both laughed as they walked up the steps to the house. When they stepped inside, Mia turned to him, and he sucked in his breath at the sadness flickering in her eyes. "You're so lucky, Lucas, to have a family that loves each other and enjoys being together."

He swallowed and reached for her hand. "You'll have that, too, someday."

"Maybe," she said and then turned and climbed back in the car.

He closed the door for her and headed to the driver's side. As he rounded the back of the vehicle, he stopped and clenched his fists at his side. The longer he was around Mia, the more his old feelings for her were emerging, but he'd seen no indication that she felt the same way. She'd gone so far as to tell him they couldn't be friends.

He took a deep breath and squared his shoulders. This day had been filled with a lot of excitement. They'd been shot at from a speeding car and found a woman's body in her home. Maybe the best thing would be to call it a day, go home and get some rest.

With that decision made, he climbed back in the car and drove toward his parents' place. "I didn't sleep well last night," he said. "I'm going to take you by my parents' home and see if my mother's there. If she is, you can stay with her, and I'll go on to my house to get some rest."

She glanced at him and nodded. "Okay, if that's what you want to do."

Lucas concentrated on the traffic as he drove but glanced at Mia from time to time. She had her head turned and stared out the window. She didn't speak on the entire ride. When they pulled into the driveway, she swiveled in her seat.

"Are you coming in?"

"Yes, I'll check…" The ringing of his cell phone interrupted him, and he pulled it from his pocket. "Hello."

"Mr. Knight, this is Janet Williams at Shackleford's Imports. I hope I'm not catching you at a bad time."

"No, Ms. Williams. It's fine."

"I got an email from my friend in London and thought you would be interested in what he told me."

"It's Janet Williams," he whispered to Mia.

Her mouth formed a small O, and her eyes grew wide. He turned his attention back to the phone. "And what did he say?"

"As you know, I had described the pieces of jewelry I saw. He said it sounded very much to him like a collection of artifacts that were unearthed in England a year or so ago. They were digging to put in a foundation for a building and discovered the remains of a house with some earthenware containers filled with coins and gold jewelry buried underneath it. This was in an area where a Roman settlement had been destroyed by the locals about AD 61, and the theory is that the owners of the house had buried the jewelry and coins for safekeeping. The treasure was taken to a local museum, but the museum was broken into about six months ago, and the pieces were stolen."

"So, does he think the pieces you saw could be the missing Roman treasure from England?"

"He didn't know, but he sent me a picture that had been circulated on the internet in an attempt to get the word out about the theft. I've looked at it, and I'm certain that the jewelry and coins I saw are the same as the ones in the picture."

Lucas exhaled a deep breath. "Then how do you think those pieces made it into the possession of Kyle Lockhart?"

"I can't say for sure, but remember how I said that I thought Mr. Lockhart traveled for work more than was necessary? If I'm remembering right, I think he was on a trip in England six months ago."

Lucas raked his hand through his hair and bit down on his lip. "Janet, where are you now?"

"I'm at work."

"Listen carefully to me. Forward a copy of that email to me, print off a copy for yourself, and take it to the police station now. You need—"

"I can't go right now, Mr. Knight. I'm the only one here at the showroom."

"Then close the showroom and get to the police station right away. I've just come from Christine Abbott's home, and she's been murdered. If the killer knows you've gotten this information, you are in danger. Now do as I say and get out of there as soon as you can."

"Okay, I just forwarded the email to your address, and I'm making the copy right now. Then I'm on my way."

"Good. Call me as soon as you get to the police station." He disconnected and stared at Mia. "It looks like Kyle was an international thief and smuggler. Let's go inside, and I'll tell you all about it."

She started to open the door but turned back to Lucas. "You sounded worried when you told Janet to get to the police as soon as possible. Do you think she's in danger, too?"

Lucas gave a curt nod. "These people killed Kyle, Clyde Harper and Christine Abbott and have tried to kill you several times. I think at this point that anybody who's connected to this case is in serious danger. I just hope these killers can be stopped before somebody else dies."

Mia could hardly believe what she was hearing as Lucas relayed what Janet Williams had told him on the phone. Her mouth gaped open as she listened and glanced across the kitchen table at Lucas's mother, who seemed just as stunned as she was. When he'd finished, no one spoke for a moment, and then she cleared her throat.

"So Janet thinks the jewelry and coins are the ten-million-dollar treasure that was stolen from a museum in England?"

Lucas nodded. "She does. Remember, Clyde was about to tell me something about smuggling when he was shot. Maybe Kyle and Chapman worked together. And…"

"Kyle and Christine got greedy and tried to keep the coins and jewelry for themselves," Mia added.

"And when Chapman found out, he killed Kyle," Lucas finished for her.

"But," Mia held up a finger to interrupt him, "Kyle had already hidden the treasure."

"And Chapman thought you might know where it was," Lucas said.

"So that's why he came after me." Mia crossed her arms and sat back in her chair.

Mrs. Knight got up and grabbed the coffeepot. As she poured more coffee in their cups, she glanced at Lucas. "Do you really think that's what this case is all about? A falling-out among thieves over some smuggled antiquities?"

He shrugged. "It makes sense. But right now it's just a theory. We won't be able to prove anything unless we can find where Kyle hid that treasure." He clasped his hands in front of him on the table and leaned closer. "Mia, can you think of any place he might have put it?"

She shook her head. "I've racked my brain for days trying to think. Evidently it wasn't at the house, or Clyde would have unearthed it. Maybe Tony found it at Christine's house."

"Maybe so, but I doubt it," Lucas said. "From the conversation Janet overheard, it seemed like Kyle was the one who came up with the hiding place—a place even Christine didn't know about." He pulled his cell phone from his pocket, and a frown wrinkled his forehead as he stared at it. "Janet has had time to get to the police station. I told her to call me."

"Don't worry," Mia said. "She may be talking with the police. Why don't you call her?"

Lucas started to punch in her number but hesitated and then shook his head. "No, I don't want to disturb her if she's talking with the police. I'll just wait."

Thirty minutes later they were still sitting at the table waiting for Janet's call. Mia pushed back from the table, picked up her coffee cup and walked to the sink. As she set the cup down, her gaze drifted down to the jeans she'd been wearing all day. For the first time she spotted a rip right below her knee.

She bent over and examined the tear better. "Would you look at that? I've torn my jeans, and they're new."

Lucas stared at it over the rim of his cup and then set it in the saucer. "Probably happened when we skidded across that pavement. Did you hurt your knee when you fell?"

She shook her head. "No. Just my jeans. I think I'll go upstairs and change. It won't take but a minute. I want to find out what the police said about Janet's information."

Hurrying upstairs, she quickly changed clothes and folded the torn pair of pants in her suitcase. She turned to leave the room, but she stopped as her gaze fell on the one-eyed Teddy sitting on the bedside table.

The toy that had brought her so much comfort in her childhood stared back at her, his one eye seeming to bore a hole through her. She sat down on the edge of the bed, reached out and picked him up. Cuddling him in her lap, she felt herself tearing up.

Since coming to the Knights' home, she'd been immersed in Christmas decorations and talk of presents, family, memories and the promise of a celebration on Christmas morning. She wondered what it would have been like to grow up where people loved each other and made Christmas a special time for friends and family. Or to have had a husband who wanted to establish new family traditions and make happy memories with his wife and children.

Teddy represented the one happy Christmas memory that she had, the last one she'd spent with her mother. She would never have what the Knights had. She could have been a part of their family, but she'd lost that chance. And it never would come again.

Tears poured down her cheeks, and she buried her face in Teddy's stubby fur. As she pulled him closer, something tickled her nose, and she drew back to get a closer look. A white thread stuck out from under his left arm. She stared at the thread for a moment before she raised his arm to get a better look.

The seam where his arm was attached to his body had a small gap in it where the stitching had come loose. She hadn't noticed the tear before.

The closer she looked, the more puzzled she became. She lifted the other arm, but the stitching there appeared intact. Frowning, she moved the bear's left arm again and realized as she moved it about, the arm became looser from the body. Had the bear's arm been damaged when Clyde had ransacked her house?

She shook her head. That didn't make sense. The seam looked as if it had been hastily sewn back together with a thread that didn't match the color of the bear. She had no idea what had happened to the toy, but she needed to fix it. Maybe Mrs. Knight had some thread and a needle she could use to do the repair.

Carefully, she pulled the white thread, and it began to unravel around the bear's arm. With a slight tug, the bear's arm detached from the body. As she tugged the arm free, some of the stuffing also came loose and rolled out. Mia picked it up and, with the tip of her index finger, pushed it back inside the bear's body. As she did, her finger touched something cold, and she realized it was metal.

She frowned and wiggled her finger around,

trying to touch the metallic piece inside the bear's body. Her fingernail hooked on a groove of some kind, and she pulled her finger out of the bear's armhole. Her eyes widened in surprise at the sight of a key sticking out.

Within seconds she'd pulled the key out and was holding it in her hand. She'd seen this object before. The last time was right before Kyle was killed. It had been where it hung every day—on a wall hook next to the back door of the kitchen. What was it doing inside Teddy now? The answer came to her in a flash, and she gasped.

She closed her fingers around the key, jumped up from the bed and ran to the stairs. As she burst into the kitchen, she stopped short at the sight of Lucas grasping the edge of the counter with one hand while the other held his cell phone to his ear. A horrified expression covered his face.

"Thank you for calling," he said. "Tell her husband we're so sorry and to call me when she's out of surgery."

He ended the call and lifted tortured eyes to Mia. Her breath hitched in her throat as she inched forward. "Who was that?"

Lucas swallowed. "The police. They wanted me to know that Janet Williams was found shot and left for dead in the parking lot behind Shackleford's. She must have been attacked when she was leaving to go to the police."

"But she's not dead?"

He shook his head. "No, she's in critical condition but was conscious enough to ask the police to call me. They've called her husband, and he's on his way to the hospital." He took one step toward Mia, and she almost gasped at the anguish on his face. "I thought when I left the navy I was through seeing people die violently, but I'm not, Mia. Janet was only trying to help me get to the bottom of this case, and now I've caused her to be hurt. I don't want to be the reason she dies." He closed his eyes and turned away from her.

Without saying anything she walked over and stopped next to him. When she put her hand on his arm, she felt his muscles contract at her touch. "This wasn't your fault, Lucas. It's Tony's. And Kyle's, for bringing this trouble into Shackleford's in the first place. He brought pain and trouble to everybody he encountered. He's hurt me enough in the past, but I don't want to see you beating yourself up over what he's done. You can't take on the responsibility for someone else's actions, and you can't let it bring you down. You're too good to let him have any effect on your life."

A sad smile pulled at his lips as he turned and faced her. Reaching up, he trailed his fingertips down her cheek. "You're beginning to sound more like that Sugar Plum Fairy I knew in college, not the scared woman who showed up on my porch a few days ago."

Mia took a big breath. "If I am, it's because you've helped me remember who I was then, and I can never thank you enough for that. But right now we have something else to do. We need to see if our theory about Kyle and Tony smuggling the stolen artifacts into this country is true. And I think I know how we can prove it."

Lucas arched an eyebrow and stared at her. "And how is that?"

She held up the key she had clasped in her hand. "I think I know where Kyle hid the treasure."

ELEVEN

Lucas frowned as he concentrated on the key Mia held in her hand. Then he glanced up, and the frown quickly disappeared as he saw that she was practically bouncing from foot to foot. "A key? Where did you get it?"

"I noticed Teddy's arm was loose, and when I examined him, I found that it had been detached and clumsily sewn back on. Then I found this key stuffed in his chest."

Lucas looked back down at the key. "And you recognize it?"

"I do," she practically squealed. "It's the key to Kyle's locker at the gym where he worked out every morning. He kept it on a key ring next to the back door. When he'd leave the house going to the gym, he'd grab it off the hook and then replace it when he came back to shower before going to work."

She handed the key to him, and he turned it

over in his hand as he examined it. "When did you last see it?"

She shrugged. "I've been trying to think, but I don't remember seeing it on the hook after he was killed."

"And you think he may have hidden the key inside your bear for safekeeping?"

She crossed her arms and nodded. "The morning of the day he was murdered, he was coming in from working out when I got up at about 6:00 a.m. He didn't usually go that early, but the gym is one of those places where VIP members have their own keys and can access the facility at any time. The strange thing was, though, he didn't look like he'd been working out. No sweat. His hair was not tousled like it always was when he got home. When I asked him why he'd gone so early, he growled that he didn't have to answer to me, and he drew back his hand like he was going to slap me. I cringed, and he just laughed and walked out of the room. I was so terrified that I would make him angry that I didn't move from the kitchen until I saw him walk out that back door."

Lucas's chest tightened at the pain flickering in Mia's eyes. He wanted to take her in his arms and tell her that he would never let anything like that happen to her again, but he didn't think she'd welcome that. Instead he balled his hands into fists and cleared his throat. "And you never saw him hang the key up?"

"No. Not when he came in and not when he left. And I was in the kitchen the whole time." A frown flashed across her face. "But come to think of it, he didn't have his gym bag when he came in. He always had it and gave me the same strict instructions about how he wanted his workout clothes laundered every time. But not that morning. He didn't mention it, and I was so eager for him to leave for work that I didn't bring up the subject."

Lucas stared down at the key again. "Have you heard from the gym since he died?"

She nodded. "I received a short condolence message from them, and they told me I could come by and clean out his locker any time I wanted to. His dues were paid up until the end of the year. I thought I could care less about what was inside that locker, but now I think it's something we need to look at."

Lucas took a deep breath. "Me, too. Let's go."

They turned to leave, but Lucas's mother appeared in the door, blocking their path. "Where are you two off to now?"

Lucas held up the key and quickly explained

to his mother where they were going. "We shouldn't be long. Then we may run by the hospital to check on Janet."

His mother looked at her watch. "Try not to be late for dinner. I'm cooking for the whole family tonight, and I expect you both to be here."

Lucas nodded. "We'll be back."

He reached out to grab Mia's arm and guide her through the door, but she pulled her arm loose and took a step backward. He glanced around at her, and her face had turned pale. "The whole family?" she rasped. "I shouldn't be here for that."

Before Lucas could speak, his mother walked over to Mia and put her arm around her shoulders. "Of course you should be here. Your being here for the past few days has reminded me of why we were so fond of you when you and Lucas were dating. This is just dinner. No big deal. Now go search that locker and come back. Claire and Jessica have been working on the nursery for the new baby all afternoon, and I may need your help getting dinner on the table."

Mia's chin quivered, and Lucas spotted a tear roll slowly out the corner of her eye. She wiped it away before she reached out and hugged his mother. Lucas felt as if he'd been hit in the chest with a sledgehammer at the sight, and he inhaled a deep breath.

Taking Mia by the arm again, he pulled her toward the door. "We'll be back for dinner, Mom."

"See you then," she called out as they headed toward the front door.

Neither of them spoke until they were in the car. Lucas had his hand on the ignition to turn it when Mia spoke up. "Your mother has been so nice to me, Lucas. I thought she would hate me."

He turned to look at her, a puzzled expression on his face. "Why did you think that?"

"Because of the way I hurt you."

He sighed and rested his elbows on the steering wheel as he stared straight ahead. Then he took a deep breath and rubbed his hands across his eyes. "Mia, why won't you believe me when I tell you that nobody hates you? All my family has ever wanted is for me to be happy, and they want the same for you."

Her lips trembled, and he could see the struggle in her face as she tried to control them. "I want that for you, too." She smiled and covered his hand with hers. "Now let's go see what's in that locker."

His skin burned where her fingers brushed his, and he huffed out a quick breath as he started the car. "You'll have to give me directions."

She laughed, and his heart skipped a beat. He glanced at her, and she looked excited, almost happy. He memorized the way she appeared at that moment and wished he could see her that way more often. With a smile, he pressed down on the accelerator and headed to the gym.

Twenty minutes later they pulled to a stop in front of a huge complex with a sign proclaiming twenty-four-hour health and fitness activities available. The parking lot appeared packed with a late afternoon crowd of customers.

Mia took a deep breath and grabbed the door handle. "Ready to go?" she asked.

"Lead the way," he said with a smile.

Together they walked into a spacious reception area that contained comfortable-looking leather couches and chairs. Pictures of men and women with perfectly toned bodies lined the walls, and Lucas couldn't help but suck in his stomach a bit as his gaze drifted around the room.

A young woman in tight-fitting spandex workout pants and top stood in back of a tall counter. A matching sweatband circled her head and looped underneath a long pony tail. She glanced up and smiled with the look of a hungry lion focused on its next meal when they approached.

"Good afternoon," she gushed as they stopped in front of her desk. "I don't think I've seen you here before. Have you come to sign up for some of our classes or just enroll in our general workout program?"

Mia smiled and shook her head. "Neither. My deceased husband, Kyle Lockhart, was a member, and I've come to clean out his locker."

The girl's eyes darkened at the mention of Kyle. "Oh, yes, I was so sorry to hear about Mr. Lockhart. He was a favorite of the staff around here. Always joking and talking with us. He had such a great personality. He must have been a wonderful husband."

Mia stiffened, and Lucas reached out and grabbed her hand. "Mrs. Lockhart has been through a terrible time, and she's trying to get all of her husband's affairs in order. So if you could just tell us where his locker is located, we'll go clean out any of his personal effects that may be in it."

The girl nodded and glanced at Mia before she directed her gaze to the computer in front of her. She clicked a few keys and looked up with a smile on her face. "His locker is number 124. It's in our VIP locker room. I'll get one of the trainers to take you down there." She picked up the phone and spoke into it. "Kane, come to the reception desk, please."

She'd barely finished speaking before the double doors to the side of her desk opened, and a guy who looked like a model for a Mr. Universe poster walked out. Lucas didn't think he'd ever seen anyone with biceps like this man had.

Kane came over to the desk. "You called for me, Nikki?"

She nodded as she pointed to Mia. "This is Mrs. Lockhart. She's here to clean out her husband's locker. It's number 124 in the VIP lounge. Can you show them the way and make sure there aren't any other clients in there right now?"

"Sure," he said. Kane grinned and motioned for them to follow him.

He led them through the gym and down a hallway with doors on either side. Stopping outside one, he turned to them. "Let me check inside before you enter."

Lucas nodded. "Thanks."

Mia fidgeted as they waited in the hall and glanced up at him from time to time. Within minutes Kane reappeared and smiled. "It's empty. Come on in."

They walked into a room lined with lockers. Off to the side Lucas could see a door with the word Sauna printed on it. Another said Weight Room. Another said VIP Indoor Track.

Lucas rolled his eyes and wondered how much a VIP membership in this club cost before he followed Kane to locker number 124. When they stopped in front of it, he glanced at Mia. "I didn't ask if you need a key."

She smiled and held up the key. "No, thanks. I have my husband's."

Her hand shook as she reached up to insert the key in the lock, and Lucas covered her hand with his. "Let me do it."

She nodded and handed him the key. He inserted it into the lock, turned it and pulled the door open. Lucas didn't know what he expected. An earthen pot with jewelry and coins piled to the rim? A leather pouch, its sides distended from the treasure enclosed within? The only thing that sat inside the locker was a nondescript gym bag. A small twinge of disappointment rippled through his body.

Mia nudged him out of the way to reach inside and pull the bag out. Then she turned to Kane, who still stood beside them, and gave him her most dazzling smile. "This is my husband's bag. I had wondered where it was. Thank you so much for helping us today."

Kane smiled, and his cheeks flushed a bit. "No problem, Mrs. Lockhart. If there's anything else you need, let me know."

"I will. Now I think we need to get going." She turned to Lucas. "Are you ready to leave? We don't want to be late for dinner."

Lucas let his gaze drop to Mia's hand that grasped the handle of the bag before he looked up into her eyes. There was an urgency in her expression that told him they needed to go. He put his hand on the small of her back and turned her toward the door. "You're right. Let's go."

They exited the lounge and walked with Kane back to the main gym, thanking him once again before they walked out to the reception area and stopped at Nikki's desk. Mia smiled again. "Thank you for being so helpful today, Nikki. Maybe after the first of the year, I'll buy my own membership in the gym. It might do me good to work out a few times a week."

Nikki didn't miss a beat as she slid a pamphlet across the desk. "Here's some information on our prices and the different programs we have. If you have any questions, just call and ask for me. I'll be glad to help you."

Mia took the pamphlet and let her gaze drift over it before she looked back up at Nikki. "I'll do that. And thank you again."

"You're welcome, and have a merry Christmas," she called out as they walked through the door to the parking lot.

Once outside they increased their gait until they arrived back at Lucas's car. Then they climbed inside, and Mia positioned the bag on her lap. Lucas's heart pounded. "Well, I guess we should check and see if we were right."

Mia nodded, slowly unzipped the bag and pulled it open. She reached inside and drew out a pair of shorts and a T-shirt that lay on top and then peered down to see what was left. A soft gasp escaped her lips. "Oh, my."

Lucas leaned closer, and she pushed the bag toward him until he could see what lay on the bottom. A smile curled the corner of his mouth and slowly spread across his face. Then he threw his head back against the headrest as laughter rolled from his throat. "I don't believe it," he gasped as he stared down at the gold jewelry and coins. "We've found the stolen Roman artifacts."

Mia pulled out matching gold earrings and held them up to her ears. Her eyes sparkled with excitement, and her cheeks were flushed.

He didn't think she had ever been more beautiful. "How do I look?" she asked.

His gaze drifted over her face. "Like a Roman goddess," he said. Then he placed his hands on either side of her face and pulled her to him until their lips touched.

He heard the earrings drop back into the bag, but he couldn't pull away from her. Then her arms looped around his neck and her fingers locked into his hair as she pulled him closer.

Mia couldn't believe this was happening. She and Lucas were sitting in the parking lot of the fitness center kissing, and she realized they were pouring all the hurt, the loneliness and the anger of the past seven years into this moment. The thought was sobering, and she pulled away.

She sank back in her seat, and Lucas crossed his arms on the steering wheel and buried his face in them. After a moment he straightened and took a deep breath. He turned to face her, and Mia almost cringed at the sadness in his eyes.

"I'm sorry, Mia," he finally said. "But I can't go on pretending that your presence these past few days hasn't affected me. It has. A lot. I convinced myself years ago that I was better off without you, but I can't lie to myself anymore. There's never been anyone in my life who starts to compare with you, and I have to tell you that I've always loved you. I'm sorry if that upsets you, but I wanted you to know."

He reached for the ignition, but she put her hand on his to stop him. "Lucas, I'm not upset. I'm happy. In fact those are the sweetest words I've heard in years. And deep down I've always known I still loved you, but I wouldn't let myself even think that there would ever be a chance for us to work things out."

He turned to face her, and the hope that blazed in his eyes pierced her heart. "What about now?" he asked. "Do you think we could?"

She shook her head. "I don't know. The years have damaged me, and I'm afraid I can't ever be the woman you deserve. I want something better for you."

He reached over and tucked a strand of hair behind her ear and touched her cheek in a soft caress. "There's no one better than you. We deserve some happiness. Don't we?"

She closed her eyes and nodded. "We do, but I'm not sure I can ever make you happy. I'm afraid I would only prove a disappointment to you."

He closed his fingers around hers and brought her hand to his mouth. She tingled all over when he pressed his lips to her palm. "You could never disappoint me. Just promise me one thing."

"What?"

"Promise me that you won't close the door on us. Think about it, and when this hunt for Tony Chapman is over, we can talk about how we go about working out our problems. Can you do that?"

She wanted to refuse, but the pleading look he directed at her wouldn't let her. After a moment she nodded. "I can do that. We'll talk later."

Lucas smiled and started the car. "Good. That's all I'm asking right now."

Mia pulled her seat belt tight and settled back in her seat as Lucas maneuvered out of the parking lot. When he didn't turn in the direction that led downtown, she swiveled to face him. "I thought we were going to police headquarters to turn this evidence in."

"We are, but I need to make a short detour first."

"Where are we going?"

He glanced at her, and a shy smile tugged at his mouth. "Tomorrow is the day the sanitation workers pick up the trash on my street. I always put Mrs. Peterson's garbage can out for her and bring it back in at the end of the day. I try to get there before dinner, so she won't worry about it. So we'll just go by and get that done, and I can put mine out, too, while I'm there."

A heaviness filled her chest at his words. How like Lucas to remember that he had a responsibility to an elderly neighbor even when it wasn't a convenient time for him. He truly was the best man she had ever known. She turned to stare out the window and placed her hand over her chest as if to keep her heart from breaking at the regret for past choices.

Neither of them spoke until Lucas pulled to a stop in his driveway. "I'll only be a few minutes," he said as he climbed out of the car.

Mia nodded and watched him roll his garbage can to the end of his driveway and then run across the street to Mrs. Peterson's house. The elderly woman came to the front door and waved when he'd pushed her can down.

"Thanks, Lucas," she yelled.

He glanced at Mia waiting in the car and walked back to where Mrs. Peterson stood. They talked for a few minutes, and then he was back in the car. He smiled at her as he started the car and was about to back out of the driveway when his cell phone chimed that a text message had just arrived. He pulled his phone out and grinned when he saw the message.

"Mom wants to know if we found what we were looking for at the gym."

"Text her back and tell her we're just leaving to go to the police."

Lucas nodded, and his fingers tapped out the quick message. He was about to put the phone back in his pocket when it chimed again. He grimaced as he read the message, and then looked up at Mia.

"She needs me to come by the house for a minute before we go downtown."

Mia frowned and leaned over to try to get a better view of the message. "Did she say what she wanted?"

Lucas shook his head. "No, but she doesn't text often. So when she does, I know it's important." He glanced at his watch. "I'd better go see what she wants."

"I think I'll stay with her to help with dinner while you take the jewelry to the police. That is, if it's okay with you."

He smiled, and her heart pounded. "I think that's great. I want you and my mother to get to know each other better."

She wanted that, too. While she'd waited

for Lucas to go to Mrs. Peterson's house, she'd thought about their conversation earlier in the gym parking lot. She still wasn't sure they could ever have a relationship, but the first glimmer of hope had begun to cast a glow in her soul.

She settled back in the seat and smiled all the way to the Knights' house. When they pulled into the driveway, Lucas glanced around and frowned. "Dad's not home yet. He was going to do some work at the agency this afternoon but said he'd be home way before dinner."

Lucas jumped from the car and appeared at her door before she had time to grab the handle. He pulled the door open, and she handed him the gym bag. "We don't need to leave this in the car," she said. Taking the bag from her, he smiled and reached for her hand. She stared up into his eyes for a moment before she placed her hand in his. With a smile on his lips, he laced their fingers together and led her toward the house.

The Christmas lights on the front porch had already been turned on, and Mia glanced up at Lucas as they stopped in front of the door. "Your mother invited me for Christmas. Do you want me to come?"

He squeezed her fingers tighter and smiled. "If you're not here, I'll come looking for you."

They laughed and walked inside. The smell

of baking bread drifted through the air, and Mia's stomach growled. Lucas bumped her shoulder with his and grinned. "Hungry?"

"Starved," she said.

He leaned over and touched his lips to her forehead. "I love a woman with a healthy appetite," he whispered as he pulled back. Then he glanced toward the kitchen. "Mom, where are you?"

His mother's soft voice answered. "I-I'm in here, Lucas."

Mia's stomach clenched at the frightened tone of Mrs. Knight's voice, and Lucas dropped her hand as he stormed toward the kitchen. At the door he stopped suddenly, and Mia plowed into his back.

A chuckle reached her ears, and the breath left her body. She'd heard that voice before. She peeked around Lucas and struggled to keep her knees from collapsing. Mrs. Knight sat in one of the kitchen chairs.

Tony Chapman stood behind her with a gun pointed to her head.

Mia gasped and took a step back but turned when something nudged her in the back. She glanced over her shoulder and grasped Lucas's arm when Donnie Miller raised his hand and pointed a gun at her head.

TWELVE

Lucas's knees trembled so hard he felt they might collapse at any moment, and he grabbed at the doorjamb to keep from falling. His gaze locked onto the gun in Chapman's hand, and he stared at it, almost unable to believe what he was seeing. A small cry escaped his mother's throat, and he blinked.

"I'm so sorry, Lucas," she said as a tear ran down her cheek. "They used my phone to text you that message. I would never have called you back here to see this."

He tried to shake the image of his mother's face from his mind, but he couldn't. He put his arm behind him to shield Mia against his back, but she leaned against him. "Lucas," she whispered. "Look over your shoulder."

Reluctantly he pulled his gaze away from his mother's face and peered back at her. His heart plummeted to the pit of his stomach when he saw Donnie Miller with a gun pointed to Mia's head. Struggling to control the rage that had begun to flow through his body, he turned forward again. "What do you want, Chapman?"

Tony laughed. "What do you think I want? What I've been looking for ever since I had to kill that two-timing Kyle Lockhart." He glanced down at the gym bag in Lucas's hand. "And I think you've just brought it to me."

Lucas glanced down at the bag he was holding. "All right. If that's what you want, let my mother and Mia go, and you can have the bag."

The corner of Tony's mouth lifted in a smirk. "Oh, I'm going to get it, but I'm not sure yet what's going to happen to these two lovely ladies you seem to care so much about." His face dissolved into a grim mask of hatred as he glared at Mia. He turned his head so that Lucas could get a good look at the red burns that streaked the side of his face. "Especially the one who did this to me. I have a score to settle with her."

Lucas's stomach clenched, and he held out the bag. "You can have this. Just let them go."

Tony glanced down at the gym bag again. "I don't think you're in a position to bargain. Now drop your gun to the floor and place the bag on the table."

Fear flashed across his mother's face, and she tried to rise from the chair. Tony grabbed her shoulder and pushed her back into the seat. "Lucas, no," she whispered. "Don't give up your gun. You know he's going to kill all of us."

Lucas hesitated a moment, unsure of what to do. He'd faced death many times when he was a navy SEAL, but he'd always had his band of brothers there with him. Now he was alone, and Chapman and Miller were threatening the lives of the two women he loved most in this world. Did he risk all their lives by giving up his gun, or did he take his chance that he might be able to get at least one shot off before Chapman or Miller could react?

Tony pressed the gun harder against his mother's head, and in the end Lucas did the only thing he could. He pulled his gun from its holster, dropped it to the floor and set the bag on the kitchen table. His mother looked up at him, a sad smile on her lips.

"I'm sorry," he whispered.

He could see tears shining in her eyes. "Don't worry, son," she said. "I understand."

Behind him he heard movement, and he turned to see Donnie holding on to Mia's arm. He pushed her past Lucas and propelled her across the room. They came to a stop next to the others. Lucas let his gaze drift over the group now facing him—Chapman with a gun to his mother's head and Miller holding one on Mia.

Donnie slipped his gun back in the waistband of his pants and glanced at Chapman. "Hold on to her while I check to see if everything's there."

Chapman reached out and wrapped his left hand around Mia's arm but still aimed the gun in his right hand at Lucas's mother. Lucas watched as Donnie unzipped the bag and threw the clothes on top to the floor. When he peered into the bottom of the bag, a big grin covered his face. The smile grew larger by the second when he reached inside and began to take inventory.

After a few minutes he nodded to Tony. "It looks like it's all here. Now take care of them and let's get out of here."

Donnie's words sent panic racing through Lucas, and his eyes grew wide. "Wait," he said. "You two have already committed enough crimes to keep you in jail for the rest of your lives. You don't need to add more to it."

"We may not need to add more to it, but we're going to," Tony seethed. "This deal wasn't supposed to take this long or have so many problems with it." He glanced at Mia. "We wouldn't be here now if it wasn't for Lockhart double-crossing us. We had a nice business going, and we were all getting rich when he decided he wanted it all. He and that Abbott woman thought they could fake a robbery of this shipment, and we wouldn't be any wiser. Too bad they were wrong."

Lucas glanced at the clock on the kitchen wall. If he could keep Chapman talking, he might be able to stall them until his father arrived home, and together they might be able to take down Chapman and Miller. He licked his lips, searched his mind for how to play for time and took a deep breath. "So it's true that you and Kyle were smuggling artifacts into the country and selling them off the books through Shackleford's Imports. How long had you been doing that?"

Tony shrugged. "Since right after old man Shackleford got sick and Kyle took over the business. I met Donnie about five years ago when we were both knocking around Europe. We ended up working for some guys in Paris who hooked us up with a smuggling ring. They set us up with a cartel that wanted access to my contacts down in New Orleans and could get the goods into the country and up the

Mississippi River to Memphis. All we needed was someone in the import business who had clients that would pay top money for one-of-a-kind artifacts."

"And that's where Kyle came in." The angry tone of Mia's voice made Lucas's breath hitch in his throat. What was she doing? She didn't need to make Chapman angrier.

"Mia…" he began, but Chapman was quicker.

He wrapped his fingers around Mia's neck and pulled upward until she was standing on her tiptoes. Her face turned red, and Lucas took a step toward her.

"Back off," Chapman ordered, "unless you want me to blow her brains out right here."

Lucas held up his hands. "Calm down. There's no need to get excited. Let go of her neck." Tony squeezed harder and then laughed as he released his hold on Mia's throat. Lucas breathed a sigh of relief and then continued. "So Kyle was your front man and sold the stolen artifacts for you. And Donnie was there at Shackleford's to help make sure that nothing showed up in the official records. You were all working together until Kyle went behind your back and…what was it you said? He pretended the shipment had been robbed?"

Donnie looked up from inventorying the contents of the bag and zipped it closed. "That's right. Lockhart and his girlfriend planned to sell it on their own. We couldn't let them do that."

Lucas glanced at the clock again. He didn't know how much longer he could keep them talking. "So you killed Christine, too?"

Chapman nodded. "I took Donnie and Clyde to her house to use her boat so Clyde wouldn't have to drive up to the front door of Lockhart's house. We didn't expect the two of you to show up. At first, it seemed like the perfect chance to grab our little troublemaker here." He gave Mia an evil grin. "But when you caught Clyde, and he decided to make a deal, I had to take care of him, too. Then I went back to meet up with Donnie at Christine's."

Donnie chuckled. "Yeah, it was kind of funny that I was holding a gun on her the whole time she stood at the door talking to the police about her boat being stolen. When they were gone, I paid her back for double-crossing us."

Lucas shook his head. "How do you guys live with yourselves? I suppose you shot Janet, too."

Donnie nodded. "Yeah, once I overheard her talking to you and realized she knew about the jewelry, she had to be taken care of. I didn't shoot to kill, just to hurt her bad enough to shut her up. By the time she's able to talk to the police, we'll be long gone. So I guess she got off lucky."

"Lucky?" Mia shouted. "The woman is badly hurt and may die, and you say she's lucky. What kind of men are you?" Lucas took a step forward as Donnie started to raise his gun.

"The kind who are about to do the same to you if you don't shut up," Donnie snarled.

Lucas held up his hands. "Calm down. There's one thing I don't understand, though. How did you guess we were going to the gym to look for the artifacts today?"

Donnie and Tony exchanged knowing glances before Tony looked at Lucas. "We figured this was the only place you'd feel safe bringing your girlfriend, and we watched until we were sure she was staying here. Then a few days ago while everybody was out, I disabled the security system and picked the lock on the back door so I could leave some bugs all over the house. We've been listening to your conversations ever since. Today we knew it had paid off because it made sense that Lockhart had stashed the loot at his gym."

Donnie pointed to the bag. "And there it is. And now it's time for us to be going." He turned to Chapman. "I'll leave the girl to you since you have a score to settle with her. I'll get the other two."

Perspiration popped out on Lucas's forehead, and the hairs on the back of his neck stood up. He had to do something. Then he blinked as Donnie raised his gun and aimed it at him. A movement caught his eye, and his stomach lurched. A strangled cry escaped his lips as his mother pushed up from her chair.

Before he could warn her off, she launched herself at him just as Donnie pulled the trigger. He heard Mia's scream, but it sounded as if it came from far away. He was only conscious of his mother's body jerking at the impact of the bullet ripping through her. With a muffled cry she collapsed against Lucas. He wrapped his arms around her and cradled her body against his. With a thud they tumbled to the floor.

The sound of the bullet still ringing in his ears, time stood still for him, and he felt himself spiraling into the mind-set of the well-trained combat SEAL he'd once been. Before he had time to think, once again he was on the battlefield, and the survival of those around him depended on what he did next. In one swift movement he scooped up his gun, which lay a few feet away, and fired off two rounds.

Donnie's eyes opened in shock as the two

bullets found their mark, and the gun dropped from his hand. His eyes glazed, and then he fell to the floor.

Lucas turned the gun on Chapman, but Chapman held Mia in front of him. His left arm circled Mia's waist with the gym bag dangling from his hand. The right one still held the gun next to Mia's head.

"I'm leaving now, Knight, and if you come after me, I'll kill her."

Mia's frightened eyes appeared locked on his mother's figure, and a tear rolled down her cheek. "Take care of your mother, Lucas," she said.

And then Chapman pulled her backward, and she was gone.

Lucas heard the front door burst open and running footsteps. He'd just pulled out his cell phone when his father ran through the kitchen door. His mouth gaped open, and he dropped to his knees next to his wife.

"What happened?"

Lucas shoved the phone in his hand. "Call 911. We need an ambulance and the police. Tony Chapman has taken Mia."

He knelt beside his mother and laid her on the floor. "Mom," he whispered. "You're going to be okay."

She opened her eyes and smiled. "Go after Mia." Her voice was so weak he could hardly hear her, and tears filled his eyes. His mother frowned. "Go, before he gets away," she murmured. Then she closed her eyes and drifted into unconsciousness.

Tears stung his eyes, and Lucas leaned over and kissed her forehead before he jumped to his feet and ran to the back door. He looked back at his mother once before running outside. His dad was with his mom, and he had to hurry. Mia's life depended on it.

The moment Tony Chapman pulled her out the back door, he stuck the gun to her head again. "My car is parked at the end of the street in the cul-de-sac," he muttered. "Don't make a sound or I'll kill you before we get there. And then I'll go back inside and kill your boyfriend."

Mia's heart pounded as if it was about to burst, and all she could do was stare at him wildly and nod. He tightened his grip on her arm and started around the house to the street, but he ducked against the house and yanked her to him when a car pulled into the driveway.

Muttering under his breath, Tony dragged her back the way they had come and headed behind the home. "This way. We'll go through the backyards to get to my car," he whispered as he propelled her toward the house next door.

As they ran behind the neighbor's house, Mia blinked at how brightly lit the backyards were from the Christmas lights on all the neighborhood houses. In the distance she heard sirens, and she knew Lucas had been able to call 911. She stared up into the sky as Tony half dragged her across the yard and prayed that help would reach Lucas's mother before it was too late.

Suddenly a large German shepherd dog ran off the back porch of the neighboring house and rushed at them, his teeth bared and his bark splitting the air. Mia gasped in horror as she saw Tony raising the gun at the approaching dog. She screamed and slammed her body against his before he could pull the trigger. The impact knocked him off balance, and he fell to the ground. The gym bag that he'd been holding flew from his grasp and landed a few feet away from him. The dog came to a stop and stood nearby growling, his hackles raised as if daring Tony to rise.

Tony didn't take his eyes off the dog as he slowly pushed to his feet. His face contorted with rage as he turned to Mia and raised the gun. "You've gotten away from me for the last time." She held up her hands in front of her face as if that could ward off the bullet he was about to fire. Before he could, a voice yelled out.

"Mia! Where are you?"

She whirled around in relief. "Lucas! I'm over here."

The sound of Lucas's voice startled Tony, and he paused as if unsure what to do. He glanced at Mia and the dog standing beside her and then to the gym bag he'd dropped. Then he scooped up the bag and ran in the direction of his car. Mia caught a glimpse of Lucas as he charged by her in pursuit of Tony, who had just discovered that a six-foot chain-link fence separated the house with the dog from its next-door neighbor.

When he was about two or three feet away, Tony threw the bag over the fence and took a flying leap toward it. His fingers latched on to the wire, and he stuck his foot about halfway up in one of the links. Then, grabbing the top of the fence with one hand, he pulled himself into a half squat on the bar at the top and prepared to jump.

"Stop, Chapman!" Lucas yelled. "You can't get away. The police are all over the neighborhood."

Tony hesitated only for a moment before he

glanced over his shoulder, raised his gun and pointed it at Lucas. Mia screamed as a gunshot echoed in the night air, and she watched in horror as Tony Chapman's hands slipped from the top of the fence and he fell to the ground.

Two policemen ran by her toward Lucas, and the three of them walked over to Tony. Mia sank down on the ground, and the German shepherd lay down beside her, his head resting on his paws. She reached over and patted him.

Finally Lucas turned and walked toward her. She stood and waited for him to approach, unsure of what she should do. "Is Tony dead?" she asked.

He stopped and stared at her. "No. The officers have called for an ambulance."

She didn't know whether to walk toward him or wait for him to come to her. At the same time they both took a step, and he wrapped her in his arms and crushed her to him as if he never wanted to let her go.

She buried her face in his chest, and after a moment he placed his fingertip underneath her chin and tilted it up. "Did he hurt you?" The hoarse words sounded as if they'd been ripped from his throat.

"No," she murmured and cupped his jaw in her palm. "Are you all right?"

"I was so scared. First my mother with a gun pointed at her, and then you. I felt like I'd been stabbed through the heart," he whispered as he turned his mouth to her palm and brushed his lips across it.

She smiled. "But you came for me anyway. That's just one more reason why you are the best man I've ever known."

Then his gaze raked her face as if trying to convince himself she was really unhurt, and he groaned before he pressed his lips to hers in a kiss that seemed an attempt to purge all the regret, hurt and anger of the years they'd been separated.

When they finally pulled apart, she stared up at him. "How's your mother?"

He shook his head. "I don't know. Dad is with her. Let's go see."

Beside them, the dog whined, and Lucas reached down to pat him. "Good boy, Brutus. The neighborhood always feels safer when you're on duty."

The back door of the house where Brutus had run from opened, and a woman hurried onto the back porch. She pulled the sash of the robe she wore tighter and stopped in shock at the sight of the police in her backyard. Her frightened gaze landed on Lucas. "Lucas, what's going on out here?"

"It's okay, Mary," he called out to her. "Brutus just helped stop a murder in your backyard."

Brutus licked Lucas's hand and then ran toward the woman on the back porch. She knelt when he bounded up the steps and wrapped her arms around the dog. "Sounds like you're a hero," she said.

Lucas smiled and nodded in agreement, then put his arm around Mia's waist and held her close as they turned and hurried back to his parents' house. The first thing Mia saw when they walked in the back door was Lucas's sister, Jessica, standing in the middle of the kitchen. Ryan was holding her in his arms while tears streamed down her face. When she saw Lucas, she pulled away from her husband and, with a squeal of relief, launched herself at her brother.

Lucas released Mia and grabbed Jessica as the two wrapped their arms around each other and rocked back and forth in a tight embrace. After a moment Lucas looked down at her. His gaze raked the kitchen. "Where's Mom?"

"They just left with her."

He swallowed, and his Adam's apple bobbed up and down. "How is she?"

Jessica's eyes filled with tears. "I don't think it's good, Lucas. Dad went in the ambulance with her. Ryan and I arrived right after Dad, and he told us you had just run out the back door after Tony Chapman. One of the officers came by a few minutes ago and told us what happened. I was so worried about you."

He smiled down at her. "Well, I'm okay. Where are Adam and Claire?"

"They're meeting us at the hospital. Ryan and I were waiting for you to come back."

He glanced at Mia and held out his hand. "Then we need to get going." Mia stepped up beside him, and he wrapped her hand in his.

Jessica glanced down at their clasped hands, wiped at the tears rolling down her cheeks and smiled. "Mia, you've been through a bad time these past few days. I'm glad it's over for you."

Mia shook her head and blinked back tears. "It won't be over until I know your mother is going to be all right."

Lucas's hand tightened on hers, and she felt a tremor run through his fingers. He inhaled a deep breath and glanced at the two EMTs who were tucking a blanket around Donnie Miller, who lay on a gurney.

"How is he?" Lucas asked.

"He's stable, so we're taking him to the hospital."

Lucas started to say something, but the back door opened, and two policemen walked inside. One of them held the gym bag. "Chapman's on his way to the hospital, and we've recovered the evidence you told us about. Looks like these guys are going to have a long string of charges against them."

Lucas turned to Mia and smiled. "Did you hear that? You're finally out of danger." He pulled her toward the door. "Now let's get to the hospital and check on my mom."

Mia nodded and let herself be guided outside to the car. All the way to the hospital neither she nor Lucas spoke, and she wondered what he was thinking. She thought about his words, that she was out of danger, but she realized that she was now in danger more than ever. In danger of ruining Lucas's life by giving in to the feelings he stirred in her.

Since the day she'd met him, she had brought nothing but heartache to him. First in college, and then when she'd shown up on his doorstep again. There were other bounty hunters she could have gone to, but she'd chosen to seek out the one person she should have kept her distance from, and it might cost him his mother.

And if it did, could he ever forgive her? Even if his mother lived, every time he looked at her, Mia would be afraid he was remembering the night his mother had almost died because of her.

Lucas had had a good life before she came back into it, a life unlike anything she'd ever known. He had parents and a brother and sister who loved him. And most of all, he had a mother who had tried to sacrifice her own life so that he might live. Mia had never had anyone in her life who could teach her how to love like that, and she didn't think she could ever measure up to the standards of the Knight family.

Thoughts like this still filled her mind four hours later as she sat next to Lucas in the hospital waiting room. Police officers, all friends of the family, plus neighbors and church members had drifted in and out all night as they came to offer their sympathy and promises of prayer. Mia had sat in silence most of the time and responded occasionally when Lucas introduced her to someone.

It warmed her heart that Lucas and his family had so many people who cared enough about them. But to her it confirmed her belief that she was the outsider here. And with that thought came the awful truth she had wanted so desperately to push from her mind. Lucas deserved someone who fit in with his friends, who understood what being a part of a family meant.

Someone much better for him than she could ever be.

As if he could read her thoughts, Lucas smiled and tightened his grip on her hand that he hadn't released since arriving. She wanted to remember how he looked at this moment, and she let her gaze drift over his face to memorize every minute detail.

He opened his mouth to say something but jerked his head around when the doctor walked into the room. The entire family jumped to their feet and surrounded the doctor the minute he stopped.

Mr. Knight was the first to speak. "How is she, doctor?"

The man raked his hand through his hair and smiled. "It was tough going there for a while, but she came through the surgery fine. Thankfully, the bullet missed any vital organs before exiting through her back. We were able to get the internal bleeding stopped, and barring any complications, she should have a relatively easy recovery. We've placed her in the Critical Care Unit for the night, but if things go well, she should be in a room by tomorrow afternoon and can maybe go home in time for Christmas."

The family breathed a collective sigh of relief, and Mr. Knight held out his hand. "Thank you, Doctor, for taking care of her." His voice quivered, and Adam reached up and squeezed his father's shoulder. Mr. Knight's eyes filled with tears as he glanced around at his family. "She's the backbone of our family. I don't know what we'd do without her."

The doctor nodded. "I understand. Now, if you'll go through the door to the unit, the nurses will let you in to see her when they get her settled. But just two at time. Okay?"

"Okay," Adam answered.

As they started to follow the doctor from the waiting room, Lucas pulled Mia forward, but she tugged her hand from his and took a step back. A frown wrinkled his forehead as he turned to her. "What's the matter?"

"The doctor said you could go in two at a time. Adam has Claire, and Jessica has Ryan. You need to go in with your father."

"But I want you to go with me," he said.

She smiled, even though she felt as if she would burst into tears any minute, and shook her head. "No, it will be better if you go with your dad." She glanced down the hall in the direction his family was walking and gave him a gentle shove. "Now, catch up with them and help your dad through this."

He cast a glance at his father's back and nodded. Then he leaned over and kissed her cheek. "Thank you for being here with me. I love you, Mia."

Her vision blurred from the tears filling her eyes. "You'll never know what those words mean to me, Lucas."

He smiled down at her once more and then turned and hurried after his family. She stood in the hallway and watched until they turned a corner and disappeared from sight. She didn't move for a minute, and then, taking a deep breath, she strode past the nurses' station and didn't stop until she stood in the hospital parking lot. She spotted her car, which she and Lucas had ridden there in, and rushed to it.

Once inside where no one could see, she folded her arms on the steering wheel and surrendered to the grief pouring through her. Her life would never be the same again because Lucas wouldn't be in it.

THIRTEEN

Mia propped her hands on her hips and let her gaze drift over the kitchen. Even though Clyde Harper had destroyed nearly everything in the room, she was about to bring a semblance of order back to it.

In the week since she'd rushed from the hospital and returned to her house, she'd made a lot of progress in getting the mess cleaned up. Of course it had helped that four workers had shown up the day after she returned and said they'd been hired by the Knight Agency to help. She'd forced the thought of Lucas from her mind and welcomed their assistance, although she instructed them that the bill for their labor should be sent to her, not the agency.

She'd wanted to call and thank the Knights, but she didn't want to chance speaking with Lucas. He'd called and texted repeatedly since she'd left the hospital, but she'd ignored all of them. A few days ago she'd even turned off her phone to keep from seeing the missed calls and texts he'd been sending. It wouldn't take him long to move on, and there was no need to delay that happening.

With a sigh, she sat down at the kitchen table and opened the notebook that lay there. A smile pulled at her lips as she skimmed the list she'd made soon after coming home. Her to-do list, she'd called it. All the things she had to do before she could start to rebuild her life.

She smiled at the first one on the list: *Get a dog.*

At that moment Caesar ran into the room, took a leap and landed in her lap. The German shepherd puppy licked at her face as she hugged him close and remembered how she'd fallen in love with him at the shelter the moment she saw him. After a minute she set him down on the floor where he settled at her feet with a contented look on his face, and she directed her attention back to the list.

Number two on the list: *Contact a real estate agent about selling the house.*

As soon as she'd gotten the call from her lawyer that she had regained control of her father's money, she'd crossed that one off. The agent was eager to put a sign in the yard, and Mia had promised her it would be ready to show by next week.

That brought her to number three: *Find a building suitable for housing a dance studio.*

The real estate agent had helped with that, too. Mia hoped to be take possession after the first of the year of a building in midtown. It was already set up as a dance studio—the previous owner had moved out of town earlier in the year.

The fourth one on the list had been harder to do, but she had persevered: *Reconnect with ballet friends from the past.*

For starters, she had found her old dance teacher, who was now retired. She had introduced Mia to the artistic director of one of the leading ballet companies in the city. When Mia had revealed her desire to put some of her father's and Kyle's money to work by supporting the organization, she had become the latest philanthropist to come on board.

Number five on her list had yet to be tackled, and she planned to do that after the first of the year: *Find a new place to live.*

This house held too many bad memories, and she couldn't wait to get out of it. All she wanted was a small home with a fenced-in backyard where Caesar could run and play and where she could sit on warm summer nights without the fear that she would be in the hospital before morning.

Since returning home, she'd been to two more meetings of the abuse survivors support group at the church, and she had begun to see more and more how she'd been a victim. With the group not meeting again for a few weeks because of the holidays, she felt at loose ends and wished she could hurry up and get started on the renovation of her new dance studio.

She pushed up from the table and walked to the counter where the coffeepot sat. After pouring herself a cup of coffee, she switched on the little radio she'd bought a few days ago. As she walked back to the table, the radio came to life, and the announcer's voice filled the room.

"Merry Christmas, all you listeners out there. I hope you're enjoying this beautiful Christmas Eve in Memphis. As we continue our broadcast of favorite Christmas music, here's a familiar one. The 'Dance of the Sugar Plum Fairy' from *The Nutcracker.*"

Mia's hand shook as the tinkling sound of the music filled the air. She closed her eyes and thought back to what Lucas had said about how beautiful she was the night she'd been the Sugar Plum Fairy. Her heart squeezed in her chest. What must he think of her now, after the way she had deserted him? If only he knew it was done out of her love for him.

Suddenly Caesar jumped to his feet and barked loudly as he ran to the front door. He arrived even before the doorbell sounded, and Mia smiled. He was going to be a good guard dog after all, if he could sense that someone had stepped on the porch before they even made their presence known.

She reached down and scooped the excited dog up in her arms, expecting to see the workers who'd said they might drop by today to pick up a ladder they'd left in her garage. When she swung the door open, the smile on her face changed to an expression of astonishment. She gasped and tightened her hold on Caesar as she stumbled backward.

Her mouth gaped open at the sight of the entire Knight family standing on her front porch. Lucas faced her, the expression on his face unreadable. His mother was in a wheelchair at his side. His father, Adam and Claire, and Ryan and Jessica surrounded them from behind. But even more surprising than realizing that they were all at her house was the fact that all of them—with the notable exception of Lucas—were smiling at her. She blinked and shook her head in an effort to make sense of what they were doing here.

They waited patiently for her to speak first. She tried, but it felt as if her breath had left her body. Finally she summoned enough strength to force her voice from somewhere deep inside of her. "Wh-what are you doing here?"

At her words Lucas's face dissolved into a huge grin. "It's Christmas Eve. I told you if you didn't show up at my parents' house, I was coming for you." Without taking his eyes off her, he nodded in his family's direction. "I brought reinforcements with me in case I couldn't convince you to come home with me for Christmas."

"B-b-but..." she stammered and wanted to kick herself for sounding like a motorboat.

"Mia," his mother spoke up, "this bunch has just checked me out of the hospital, and we're on our way home. But we wanted to come tell you that we're so glad you came back into our lives. Every one of us, especially Lucas, is thankful that God has given us a second chance to be a family. And if you'll have us, we'd welcome you with open arms. On Christmas Eve we all spend the night at our house so we can be together on Christmas morning. Tonight we're having a small dinner, but tomorrow we'll celebrate all our family traditions. We want you to be a part of it."

Tears welled in her eyes, and she stared at his mother. "But why would you want me there? If I hadn't been at your house, Tony Chapman would never have come there. I'm the reason you were almost killed."

Mrs. Knight frowned and shook her head. "You can't take the blame for what that man did. But you can take the *credit* for something else you did."

Mia's eyes grew wide. "What?"

Mrs. Knight reached out and grasped Lucas's hand. "For making my son happier than he's been in years. He loves you, Mia, and I believe you love him. So that means that we love you, too. Now, how about it? Are you coming home with us for Christmas?"

Mia's lips trembled, and she glanced at each of the Knights with her gaze coming to rest on Lucas. "Do you really want me to come?" she asked.

He nodded. "We all do, Mia. Please give us a chance."

Her face crumpled, and she began to cry. "Give you a chance? I'm the one who's not worthy of all of you."

He tilted his head to one side and grinned at

her. "All I'm asking is a chance to convince you differently. Will you let me do that?"

She couldn't speak, so she only nodded.

He took a deep breath and glanced over his shoulder. "Okay, I'll take it from here. Thanks for helping me out. Take Mom on home, and we'll be there in a little while."

"See you later" rang out from the others as Adam and his father lifted the wheelchair down the steps, and they all headed to the cars.

Lucas waited until they'd driven away before he turned back to face her. "Are you going to invite me in?"

For the first time, she realized she had kept them standing on the front porch. Her face grew warm, and she stepped back for him to enter. When she closed the door, she turned to face him, still unable to believe he was actually in her house. His gaze dropped to the dog she still held.

"I see you got a dog."

She nodded. "Yes. His name is Caesar."

His eyebrow cocked, and he laughed. "Did you name him as a tribute to Brutus?"

"Yes."

He glanced at the dog again. "Are you going to put him down so I can kiss you?"

Unsure of her answer, she bent over and deposited Caesar on the floor, then did the only thing she wanted to do. She launched herself into his arms.

With Christmas dinner over, Lucas sat sprawled on the sofa with Caesar at his feet when Mia walked into the den. He didn't take his eyes off her as she sat down next to him and sighed. He put his arm around her shoulders and pulled her close. This was the perfect ending to a perfect day. He'd never felt so contented in his life, and it was all because of this woman who snuggled near him. He could feel the rhythm of her breathing, and he sighed with pleasure as he stared at the flames blazing in the fireplace.

"I just talked to Janet Williams's husband," he said. "Janet regained consciousness yesterday, and the doctors say she's going to make a complete recovery."

Mia didn't move, just stared at the fire. "I'm glad. Have you gotten an update on Tony and Donnie?"

"Ryan told me they're both recovering and should be transferred to jail soon. So you don't have anything to worry about from them. You're safe now."

She reached up and covered his hand with hers. "Thanks to you."

They both sighed and settled back into a comfortable silence, content to be together on this peaceful night. After a few minutes he turned to face her and smiled. "What are you thinking?" he asked.

She pulled her feet underneath her and snuggled closer. "I'm thinking how happy I am. I never knew Christmas could be like this. I couldn't believe it when your dad ran down the hall knocking on everybody's door this morning yelling merry Christmas."

Lucas chuckled. "Yeah. He's done that all my life." He tightened his arm around her shoulders, and his hand traced little patterns on her neck. "What else did you like?"

"Having breakfast with all of you, sitting around the Christmas tree and reading the Christmas story from the Bible, and singing carols."

He grinned. "How about your presents? Did you like them?"

She laughed and punched him on the arm. "Of course I liked the presents, but I still can't believe everyone in your family gave me something. They didn't have to do that. But my most favorite things about today were how all of you laughed together, how you showed your love for each other and how much fun you had together eating that delicious Christmas dinner Claire and Jessica cooked." She swallowed and tilted her head to stare up at him. "I've never had anything like that. I feel like this is really my first Christmas."

Lucas leaned over and kissed her forehead. "Don't worry. My family will see to it that it's not your last." He glanced over his shoulder and frowned. "Speaking of my family, where did they all go?"

"Your dad took your mom upstairs to rest. Adam and Claire went over to the next-door neighbor's house, and Jessica and Ryan are in the kitchen."

He chuckled. "I guess they wanted to give us some time alone."

Mia's eyebrow arched. "And why did they think we needed some time alone?"

He reached for her hand, and he wondered if she could tell how just her touch thrilled him. He'd thought her lost to him forever. Now they had a second chance. But he had to convince her of it.

"Mia, a lot has happened to us since we were in college. When I was a SEAL, I experienced things…things I can never tell you about. But I can't erase them from my memory. I probably never will—just as you will never be able to forget what Kyle did to you. We both have lots of baggage, but I think we can deal with it all if we do it together."

Tears glistened in her eyes. "And how do we do that?"

"The only way we can. By loving each other, and helping each other every day to remember that God is with us. I believe He has a plan for us. Maybe He had one years ago, and we messed up. But I think He's giving us a second chance to do it right this time. We need to let faith guide us, and I know He'll bless us." He ran his fingers over her knuckles. "I've always loved you, Mia. And this time I don't want to lose you. Please, tell me you're willing to give us a chance."

A tear rolled down her cheek, and he rubbed it away with his thumb. "I do love you, Lucas," she said. "I just didn't feel I was worthy of you. I wanted something better for you."

He shook his head. "You're all I want. You're all I need. Please, please, don't leave me again."

She reached up and cupped her hand around his jaw. He closed his eyes at the gentle touch of her fingers. "I do love you, Lucas. More than I can ever tell you."

"Then marry me," he murmured. "Marry me and make my lonely life finally have some meaning."

He opened his eyes, and she was smiling. "I'll marry you, Lucas. There's no one I'd rather spend the rest of my life with than you. But what about your family? Do you think they'll accept me?"

"They will. All they want is my happiness, and they know you're the one who can complete me."

He reached in his pocket and pulled out the small box he'd kept locked away in a drawer for years. "I have something for you," he said.

When he opened it, her eyes widened. "Oh, Lucas, the locket you gave me the night I danced in *The Nutcracker*. I didn't know you'd kept it."

He nodded. "When you gave it back to me after we broke up, I couldn't make myself get rid of it. Every once in a while I'd get it out and look at it. And I'd wonder what you were doing. If I had known what you were going through, I would have tried to help you."

"I know. But that's all behind us now." She glanced down at the locket. "Is our picture still inside?"

He opened it and held it out for her to see.

The picture of them, their heads touching and smiles on their faces, stared up at them. "This was made a few weeks before the performance."

"I know." She bowed her head toward him, and he fastened the locket around her neck.

"This is just to seal our commitment until we go get your engagement ring this week."

A look of panic flashed in her eyes. "Lucas, are you sure your family is okay with this?"

He laughed and tugged her to him. "They're fine. With life the way it is around here, we just roll with the punches."

She smiled as his lips brushed hers, and then she pulled his head down and pressed her lips against his. After a moment she separated and stared up at him. "Now, that's a proper kiss."

He leaned forward to kiss her again but hesitated as his sister ran into the room. "Stop, you two!" Jessica yelled. "We've got an emergency. Claire has gone into labor, and I think Adam is about to pass out. We've got to leave for the hospital right now."

Lucas laughed, grabbed Mia's hand and pulled her to her feet. "So much for Adam bragging about how he was the coolest expectant father ever."

"Well, he's not cool anymore," Jessica said.

"Mr. Always-in-Control Bounty Hunter is in a panic. Claire's suitcase is at home, and he's afraid there isn't enough gas in his car to get to the hospital."

She'd barely finished speaking when Lucas caught sight of Adam with his arm around Claire, ushering her down the hallway to the front door. "Now, don't worry, honey," Adam said. "We're gonna get through this without any trouble." He jerked the front door open. "Get in Ryan's car. He and Jessica are going to drive us."

Claire came to a stop and put her hands on her hips. "Adam, I need my coat. It's freezing outside."

His face turned pale, and he rushed toward the living room. "I'll get it."

"Adam," she called out. "It's in the kitchen."

He skidded to a halt and turned toward the kitchen. "Oh, yeah. Be right back. Don't leave without me."

Claire let out a sigh and shook her head in Mia's direction. "Now, that sounds like a good idea."

Before they could say anything, Adam came running back with two coats in his hands. He grabbed Claire's left arm and tried to force it into the sleeve of one of them, and she jerked her arm free. "Adam, that's your coat."

Lucas laughed, and Adam glared at him before he bundled both coats under one arm and grabbed Claire with his other hand. "Claire, will you please get in the car before we have to deliver this baby in the entry hall?"

Claire rolled her eyes and huffed out a big breath. "Adam, if you don't calm down, we're going to have to get you a wheelchair when we get to the hospital."

"Claire," Adam groaned, "if you don't get in the car this minute, I'm going to pick you up and put you there myself."

Claire looked over her shoulder as Adam propelled her out the door and arched her eyebrows. "Welcome to life in the Knight family, Mia. You never know what's going to happen next."

Lucas stood at the door and watched until Ryan drove away. He shook his head and laughed when he saw Adam lean over from the backseat and gesture wildly. Probably giving instructions on which route to take to the hospital. When the car disappeared down the street, he closed the door and faced Mia.

"Well, there's a preview of how quickly life

can change around here. What do you think? Are you ready to take this bunch on?"

She looped her arms around his neck and smiled up at him. "I think I'm going to enjoy every minute."

* * * * *

Dear Reader,

Yuletide Fugitive Threat was a difficult book to write because of the domestic violence that served as the basis for Mia's story. As I wrote about her experiences, I was reminded that she was not unique in what she suffered. It has been reported that each year 4,774,000 women in the United States experience physical abuse from an intimate partner and that one in four women will be victims of physical violence by an intimate partner in their lifetimes. If you or someone you know is caught in this vicious trap, I hope that you will seek help before it is too late. Don't continue to suffer because your husband or boyfriend has convinced you that you are the one at fault in the relationship. In my story, even though Mia was released from her situation, she still had a lot of healing to do. I'm praying that you, too, can find the strength to seek help that will bring complete healing into your life.

Sandra Robbins

LARGER-PRINT BOOKS!

GET 2 FREE
LARGER-PRINT NOVELS
PLUS 2 FREE
MYSTERY GIFTS

Love Inspired®

Larger-print novels are now available...

LILP15

REQUEST YOUR FREE BOOKS!
2 FREE WHOLESOME ROMANCE NOVELS IN LARGER PRINT
PLUS 2
FREE
MYSTERY GIFTS

✻✻✻✻✻✻✻✻✻✻✻✻✻✻✻✻✻✻✻✻✻✻

HEARTWARMING™

❈❈❈❈❈❈❈❈❈❈❈❈❈❈❈❈❈❈❈

Wholesome, tender romances

YES! Please send me 2 FREE Harlequin® Heartwarming Larger-Print novels and my 2 FREE mystery gifts (gifts worth about $10). After receiving them, if I don't wish to receive any more books, I can return the shipping statement marked "cancel." If I don't cancel, I will receive 4 brand-new larger-print novels every month and be billed just $5.24 per book in the U.S. or $5.99 per book in Canada. That's a savings of at least 19% off the cover price. It's quite a bargain! Shipping and handling is just 50¢ per book in the U.S. and 75¢ per book in Canada.* I understand that accepting the 2 free books and gifts places me under no obligation to buy anything. I can always return a shipment and cancel at any time. Even if I never buy another book, the two free books and gifts are mine to keep forever.

161/361 IDN GHX2

Name _____ (PLEASE PRINT)

Address _____ Apt. #

City _____ State/Prov. _____ Zip/Postal Code

Signature (if under 18, a parent or guardian must sign)

Mail to the **Reader Service:**
IN U.S.A.: P.O. Box 1867, Buffalo, NY 14240-1867
IN CANADA: P.O. Box 609, Fort Erie, Ontario L2A 5X3

* Terms and prices subject to change without notice. Prices do not include applicable taxes. Sales tax applicable in N.Y. Canadian residents will be charged applicable taxes. Offer not valid in Quebec. This offer is limited to one order per household. Not valid for current subscribers to Harlequin Heartwarming larger-print books. All orders subject to credit approval. Credit or debit balances in a customer's account(s) may be offset by any other outstanding balance owed by or to the customer. Please allow 4 to 6 weeks for delivery. Offer available while quantities last.

Your Privacy—The Reader Service is committed to protecting your privacy. Our Privacy Policy is available online at www.ReaderService.com or upon request from the Reader Service.

We make a portion of our mailing list available to reputable third parties that offer products we believe may interest you. If you prefer that we not exchange your name with third parties, or if you wish to clarify or modify your communication preferences, please visit us at www.ReaderService.com/consumerschoice or write to us at Reader Service Preference Service, P.O. Box 9062, Buffalo, NY 14240-9062. Include your complete name and address.

HW15

YES! Please send me **The Montana Mavericks Collection** in Larger Print. This collection begins with 3 FREE books and 2 FREE gifts (gifts valued at approx. $20.00 retail) in the first shipment, along with the other first 4 books from the collection! If I do not cancel, I will receive 8 monthly shipments until I have the entire 51-book Montana Mavericks collection. I will receive 2 or 3 FREE books in each shipment and I will pay just $4.99 US/ $5.89 CDN for each of the other four books in each shipment, plus $2.99 for shipping and handling per shipment.*If I decide to keep the entire collection, I'll have paid for only 32 books, because 19 books are FREE! I understand that accepting the 3 free books and gifts places me under no obligation to buy anything. I can always return a shipment and cancel at any time. My free books and gifts are mine to keep no matter what I decide.

263 HCN 2404   463 HCN 2404

Name	(PLEASE PRINT)	
Address		Apt. #
City	State/Prov.	Zip/Postal Code

Signature (if under 18, a parent or guardian must sign)

Mail to the **Reader Service:**
IN U.S.A.: P.O. Box 1867, Buffalo, NY 14240-1867
IN CANADA: P.O. Box 609, Fort Erie, Ontario L2A 5X3

READERSERVICE.COM

Manage your account online!

- Review your order history
- Manage your payments
- Update your address

We've designed the Reader Service website just for you.

Enjoy all the features!

- Discover new series available to you, and read excerpts from any series.
- Respond to mailings and special monthly offers.
- Connect with favorite authors at the blog.
- Browse the Bonus Bucks catalog and online-only exculsives.
- Share your feedback.

Visit us at:
ReaderService.com